PHANTOM LIMB

ALSO BY BRIAN EVENSON
FROM COFFEE HOUSE PRESS

NOVELS

Father of Lies

Last Days

The Open Curtain

STORIES

A Collapse of Horses

Fugue State

The Glassy, Burning Floor of Hell

Good Night, Sleep Tight

Song for the Unraveling of the World

Windeye

PRAISE FOR BRIAN EVENSON

"Brian Evenson is one of my favorite writers. The stories in this collection will thrill, unsettle, and captivate. Like lanterns in dark rooms, paper boats carried down on subterranean waters, they lead the reader into mysterious and perilous territory. Read at your own risk."

—Kelly Link

"Brian Evenson is the Donald Barthelme of psychological horror."

—*The Los Angeles Times*

"[Evenson's] writing approaches the luxurious, haunted feeling that Bradbury conjured so well. It's almost a shame to have all these stories in the same place; they shouldn't be read at once for risk of overdosing."

—Liz Braswell, *The Wall Street Journal*

"Evenson is probably your favorite horror writer's favorite horror author."

—Liberty Hardy, *Book Riot*

"Evenson's clear, fluid, perfectly balanced prose is a joy to read while deceptively simple, streamlined plots are hiding abysses of dark portents."

—Dejan Ognjanović, *Rue Morgue*

"His stories are deeply terrifying and so troubling that they linger in your mind long after you've read them."

—R. L. Stine

"A master of literary horror."

—*GQ*

PRAISE FOR BRIAN EVENSON CONT.

"Brian Evenson is one of my favorite living horror writers."

—Carmen Maria Machado

"There is not a more intense, prolific, or apocalyptic writer of fiction in America than Brian Evenson."

—George Saunders

"Like with Borges or Kafka, every one of Brian Evenson's stories are a whole world distilled down to a few pages, and rendered in a pointillism that feels not just abstract, but cosmic, yet is gritty all the same, and leaves a distinct, bloody residue in your mind, in your heart. And then you can no longer look at the world the way you used to."

—Stephen Graham Jones

"Evenson is one of our best living writers—regardless of genre."

—NPR

"Evenson's fiction is equal parts obsessive, experimental, and violent. It can be soul-shaking."

—*The New Yorker*

"Evenson has created a haunted world of violence and damage, where the more a person loses the closer they get to God... [He] proves yet again to be a master alchemist, stirring up a noir-infused detective story, a cultic conspiracy, and some wonderfully grisly body horror into a concoction that is distinctly Evenson"

—Brandon Grafius, author of *Scared by the Bible*

PHANTOM LIMB

BRIAN EVENSON

COFFEE HOUSE PRESS

Cover design by Mel Nigro

Cover art by Jeffrey Alan Love

Book design by Coffee House Press

Author photo © A. Hornischer, The American Academy in Berlin

Coffee House Press books are available to the trade through our primary distributor, Consortium Book Sales & Distribution, cbsd.com or (800) 283-3572. For personal orders, catalogs, or other information, write to info@coffeehousepress.org.

Coffee House Press is a nonprofit literary publishing house. Support from private foundations, corporate giving programs, government programs, and generous individuals helps make the publication of our books possible. We gratefully acknowledge their support in detail in the back of this book.

Library of Congress Cataloging-in-Publication Data

Names: Evenson, Brian, 1966- author
Title: Phantom limb / Brian Evenson.
Description: Minneapolis : Coffee House Press, 2026.
Identifiers: LCCN 2026018434 (print) | LCCN 2026018435 (ebook) | ISBN 9781566897686 trade paperback | ISBN 9781566897693 ebook
Subjects: LCGFT: Fiction | Novels | Detective and mystery fiction | Thrillers (Fiction)
Classification: LCC PS3555.V326 P43 2026 (print) | LCC PS3555.V326 (ebook)
LC record available at https://lccn.loc.gov/2026018434
LC ebook record available at https://lccn.loc.gov/2026018435

Printed in the United States.

32 31 30 29 28 27 26 25   1 2 3 4 5 6 7 8

It was a charcoal sketch of himself, very cleverly done, showing him reposing in a little basket. He was without arms and legs, there was a beatific, saintly expression on his face.

—Bernard Wolfe, *Limbo*

Cut a little finger,
Stick it on a postcard,
Send it to the sky,
It comes back to me.

—Tom Ellard, “Fingers”

On one of these occasions, completely furious, and resolved never again to practice magic, I cut off my hands. To no purpose. As soon as I moved, they reappeared, fresh and perfect, on the ends of the stump of each arm!

—Murilo Rubião,
"The Ex-Magician from the Minhota Tavern"

PART ONE

1.

He dreamt he met a woman at the corner bar, only he wasn't sure what corner and it didn't look like any bar he had ever seen. Its angles kept shifting and changing, as if it were a living thing. Perhaps it was.

After a while, she smiled and slid off her stool and sidled toward the exit, glancing back over her shoulder to assure herself he was following. Something was wrong with one leg. There was a slight catch to her step, nearly a limp but not quite.

He followed her along a dark, damp street in a cold drizzle, then down a pale alley. Near its end, she started up a rickety set of wooden stairs. He followed. Did we talk in the bar? *he wondered. He couldn't remember.* Do I know anything about her? *He didn't think so. He was on the stairs now and there she was, above him, on a creaking, swaying landing, forcing a window sash up. She was stronger than she looked. Once it was open, she propped it in place with a sheared-off broomstick handle that she fumbled out from somewhere inside, and then clambered drunkenly through.*

He stayed on the landing, hesitant, unsure what was expected of him. If this was really her place, why would she go in this way? What was he getting himself into?

He could barely see her within, the lesser dark of her body rustling through the greater dark of the room. She glided close to the glass of the window and beckoned to him, then faded away like a ghost.

Gathering his breath, he clambered after her.

She stood just beside a closet door. As he approached, she tugged at the knob. With a click, the door opened.

It was too dark within the closet for him to see clearly. There was something there, but he couldn't make out what. A heap of something, or a pile.

Another click, and abruptly he saw her pale white arm illuminated there beside him, its fingers still caressing the switch plate. In the sudden light, the vague heap or pile became a stark mound of shoes, as high as his breastbone.

There was something strange about the mound, something wrong. He couldn't quite say what.

He turned to stare at her.

She stood in the sharp slash of light cast from within the closet. It was easy now, in this stark light, to see what was wrong with her leg: what he had assumed to be flesh and bone was a prosthetic. Once he realized this, it was hard to look at anything else.

When, finally, he tore his gaze free, he knew what had disturbed him about the mound of shoes: all of them, all the shoes he could see and doubtless all the shoes hidden below, curved the same way. All were for the same foot.

But which foot? *he wondered.* The foot that she has or the foot that she doesn't?

Before he could decide, the mound itself began to vibrate, something not yet visible welling slowly up from within.

. . .

Kline lay there for a long while, mouth dry, staring at the ceiling. He could briefly sense his own missing arm, as if still attached, tingling. As he became more awake the sensation faded, leaving nothing but empty air.

He got up and went to the sink, pouring himself a cupful of water. Slowly, he drained the cup dry. It tasted of rust, but whether that was from the pipes or from the metal of the cup he couldn't say. Maybe both.

Who was she? he wondered. *Is her face a face I know? Is she anyone real at all?* Her face was familiar and not at the same time. Not someone from the Brotherhood, he didn't think.

It had been days since he had thought of the Brotherhood. Days since he had been sober enough to think of anything at all. Now that he was thinking again, he wished he wasn't.

He stared into the polished metal mirror. A ravaged face, smeared with badly healed wounds, strips of puckered pink flesh where he had burned, the hair on his head patchy and incomplete. He hardly looked human anymore.

He returned to the cot. He lay there, trying to fall back to sleep.

He couldn't. He stared at the ceiling, then at the cell's bars, then through them and out into the brightly lit corridor beyond.

After what felt like hours, at last a buzzer sounded and the lights within the holding cell flickered on.

An officer appeared at the end of the corridor, carrying a battered tin tray. There was an open pint of milk on it, a pressed paper bowl full of flaccid cornflakes already soaking in milk, a heap of browning apple slices. *Dawkes*, the tag pinned to his uniform read. With a grunt, the man labeled Dawkes placed the tray on the floor.

"All right," Dawkes said. "Step away from the door. Far wall. Face it. Hands against the cinder block. Stay there until I give the word."

"Hand, you mean," Kline said, and rolled his armless side toward him.

"Figure of speech," Dawkes managed after a confused pause. Then, "Don't give me that look: give it to the damn wall."

Kline did. He listened to the scrape of the key in its cradle, the click the lock made as the key turned, the slight squeal of the cell door opening, the rasp as Dawkes nudged the tray along the cement floor and into the cell with his shoe. *Is there enough time for me to turn and rush him?* Kline wondered. As he was thinking it, the cell door squealed again, clanged shut.

"Enjoy your breakfast," said Dawkes, and left.

Kline pushed off the wall, bent down to gather the tray. He grabbed it with his hand and then used his hip to help support it as he stepped back to the cot. Some of the bowl's milk slopped onto his tray and fingers.

Seated on the cot, he balanced the tray on his knees. He ate slowly, considering.

What do they know? he wondered. *Obviously not much or they would have already moved me. But enough, apparently, to be cautious.*

In the late morning someone new arrived. A small man, with dark hair running to gray at the temples. A delicately structured face that looked as though it could be easily damaged. Sharp nose, steady look. Unlike Dawkes, he didn't have a nametag, and he didn't wear a uniform.

Dawkes unlocked the cell. He let the man in while Kline stood again with his hand pressed to the wall.

Kline heard the cell door squeal shut. "At ease," the new man said, though he didn't look military. Kline turned from the wall to find the man seated on his cot, a sheaf of papers gathered on his lap. The man patted the blanket beside him. "Come, friend," he said. "Let's talk."

"I'm not your friend," Kline said.

"I'm the only friend you have at the moment," said the man. "Let's chat a bit. See where it leads us."

Kline hesitated, then awkwardly sat. The cot's springs squealed.

"Say we start with your name again," said the new man.

"Josef," lied Kline. "With an f."

"Last name?"

"Horkai."

"All right," the new man said, affably enough. "At least you're consistent. We already know that's not your name. We don't have to start with names if that's how you're going to be. Shall we start with your burns?"

"They're old burns," said Kline.

"Days old, anyway," said the new man. "Care to say where they came from?"

"I don't recall."

"You're not making this easy," said the new man. His voice seemed a little sad, though his gaze remained steady, observant. "I promise it'll just go worse for you in the long run."

No, thought Kline, *once you figure out who I am, that's when it will go much, much worse.*

"Hunted animal is the way you're acting," said the new man. "Why? Are you?"

"Hunted? By what?" asked Kline. And then added, "What kind of animal?"

The new man smirked but didn't bite. He glanced at the papers on his lap. "Says here you were squatting in a ruined house, a mile or two outside of town, up a track in the hills. Not occupied for years. Sound about right?"

"I was in a shack," Kline said. "I'm not exactly sure where it was."

"What were you doing there?"

"Gathering myself."

"For what?" asked the new man. "Or should I say *from* what?" He stared at Kline, eyebrows lifted, waiting.

When Kline didn't speak, he ruffled his papers and went on.

"Johnson place," he said. "Chet Johnson used to live there, back in the day before he hanged himself. Knew him when I was a boy. Real bastard. Your name Johnson by chance?"

"No," said Kline. "Horkai."

"Did Chet Johnson's son give you permission to use the place? Did another one of his kin?"

"No," said Kline. "I was trespassing. I willingly admit it. Charge me with trespassing."

"What did you say your name was again?"

"Horkai."

The new man frowned. "We took fingerprints," he said. "Didn't get much. Your hand is a little burnt. As in a lot burnt. Along with the rest of you."

Kline didn't say anything.

"In another few weeks the skin will grow back. Enough anyway for us to get at least one readable print."

"Probably," said Kline.

"Must have been quite a blaze," said the man.

"Must have been," agreed Kline.

"So, squatting in an empty shack. Judging from the number of empty bottles, you were there a while. How long?"

"I don't recall," said Kline.

"Lots of bandages, too," said the man. "Old gauze soaked in pus and blood. Empty pill bottles: painkillers, antibiotics. All sorts of names on the bottles. None of them *Horkai*." He gave Kline a piercing gaze. "You made your way there to hide out and heal."

Kline didn't say anything.

The man looked down at the papers again. "Lots of empty bullet casings," he said. "Scattered all over the floor. Small target painted in blood on one wall, silly with bullet holes."

"Must have happened before I arrived," said Kline, holding the muscles of his face still.

"Nice try," the new man said. "The sound of shots was what brought officers out. We did a GSR on your hand. You'd fired a gun recently. I'm willing to bet if the blood of that target was analyzed it'd turn out to be yours." The man leaned closer and grinned. "Care to tell me what a half-burnt man is doing holed up in a shack, drinking himself into a stupor while taking pot shots at a target drawn in his own blood?"

"Who says it's my blood?"

"Would it make it better somehow if it was someone else's blood?" the man asked, feigning surprise. "But yes, I know. It's definitely your blood. I had it analyzed after all. I'm thorough." His smile was cold now. "And the gun," the man said, "when we finally dug it out from under the piles of bloody gauze, turns out the registration number had been filed off."

"You don't say," said Kline.

"I do indeed say," said the man. "And then we realized—or I realized anyway—that your burnt-off fingerprints aren't all that different from the smeary prints that were left at a late-night break-in a few weeks back. Mom and Pop grocery. No cash taken, only a case of vodka. Hard to tell there'd been a break-in at all except the Mom of the Mom and Pop had just inventoried the store. She knew exactly what they had. Strange thing is, the missing case of vodka is the same brand as the empties littered around your hideout. Shall we call it your hideout?"

"Let's not," said Kline. Then he added, "There are only so many brands of vodka."

The new man ignored him. "And to top it off, when the local officers come to have a little chat with you, you decide it'd be a fine idea to resist arrest. And why not assault an officer or two while you're at it for good measure?" The man leaned back, stretched. "Anything to say yet?"

They stayed there, not blinking, regarding one another.

"Do I get a phone call?" Kline finally asked.

The new man nodded. "We're civilized folk here," he claimed. "At least for the moment."

"I'd like that phone call now," said Kline.

It took a little while to get Dawkes back to the cell, a while longer to put irons on Kline's legs and get a belly chain on and cuff Kline's hand to it. He shuffled down the hall until they reached the payphone, but when he reached awkwardly for the handset, the new man already had his hand resting on it.

"No," he said. "Tell me the number and I'll dial it."

"I can dial by myself."

The new man shook his head. "We're civilized, but not that civilized. Also, I'll be right here the whole time you talk."

"That infringes on my rights," Kline said.

"It does," agreed the man amiably. "But it's your word against mine. My word says I withdrew to a respectable distance and allowed you privacy."

Kline said nothing.

"Funny that *you're* worried about *me* doing something legally questionable," the man said. He lifted the handset, shook it. "Well? You want to make that call or not?"

When the operator came on, the new man covered the phone's transmitter with his palm and said, "Number?"

"Second Precinct," said Kline, and named the city.

For the first time, the new man seemed caught off balance. "Police precinct, you mean?"

Kline nodded.

The man nodded back, wary now, then passed the request on.

"It's ringing," he said eventually. And then, to Kline, "Who exactly should I ask for?"

"Ask for Frank," said Kline.

"Frank who?"

"They'll know who."

The new man asked. He listened, then covered the transmitter. "Pensioned off," he said. "Weeks back."

"Get his home number," said Kline.

After a certain amount of negotiation, the new man did. "We're stretching the one phone call rule a little," he said once he had it, "but what the hell? Who should I say is calling?"

Kline considered, finally said, "Tell him the man with two heads."

The connection was indifferent, a little crackly. The handset was still warm from where it had been pressed against the new man's face.

"Hello, Frank," said Kline. "Remember me?"

At the far end of the telephone line, Frank gave a bitter laugh. "How in hell could I forget?"

"I need some help," said Kline.

"Not interested."

"You're the only person I can call."

"Not my problem," Frank said. "Last time I tried to help you, look where it got me."

"This time you're perfectly safe," said Kline. "I'm in a cell."

Frank let out a barking laugh. "Finally turned yourself in, did you?"

"Not exactly," Kline said.

"They picked you up?"

"Yes."

"On what?"

"Come find out," said Kline. "Aren't you curious?"

"Why not just tell me over the phone?"

"It's delicate. I'd rather talk in person," said Kline. "Come down. Ask for Josef Horkai. What can it hurt?"

"That's exactly what I'm afraid of finding out," said Frank, and hung up.

"No luck?" asked the new man. "Nobody coming to help you sort this mess out?"

Kline shook his head. He awkwardly returned the handset to its cradle and let the new man lead him back to his cell.

2.

And yet, a few hours later, there Frank was, being led to his cell by a somewhat startled Officer Dawkes.

"What's the matter?" Frank asked Dawkes as he opened the cell door. "Never seen two one-armed men in the same jail before?" Dawkes, shaking his head, didn't bother to answer.

Frank had changed since Kline had last seen him. He had grown gaunt, the lines of his face more severe. He had lost most of his hair, and what remained was shaved close to the skull. What remained of his arm, amputated somewhere between elbow and shoulder, was hidden in the pinned-up sleeve of a denim shirt. A delicate webwork of scars was spread over his cheeks and forehead from where glass had shattered into it, just present enough to catch the light if he turned wrong.

Dawkes hurried away. For a moment, they both stared at one another. "Hello, Frank," Kline finally said. "Thanks for coming."

"Say your piece so I can leave," said Frank.

"I'm sorry about your arm."

"I'd say it wasn't your fault," said Frank, "but that would be lying. Apology not accepted."

Kline gave him an appraising look. "You don't look like the sort to hold a grudge."

"Looks can be deceptive," said Frank. He grimaced. "Last time I saw you, you were carrying one head too many. Then you decided maybe you'd leave your spare head under my hospital bed." He leaned closer. "You know what it's like knowing there's a severed head under your bed?"

"Probably unpleasant," said Kline.

"That's it?" said Frank. "No *Sorry about the head, Frank*?"

"I already apologized for the arm," said Kline.

"Last conversation we had," said Frank, "you, me, and the head, you said you wanted to turn yourself in."

"Change of heart," said Kline.

"And yet, here you are. Jailed anyway." Frank absently tried to fold his arms, seemed a little surprised to find the one missing. Abandoning the gesture, he leaned back against the bars.

"Here I am," said Kline.

"There you are," said Frank, and waited. "Well?" he finally said. "What the hell you want?"

"I was hoping you could get me out."

Frank laughed. "I bet you fucking were," he said. "Frank comes waltzing in and pulls a few strings attached to his cop friends and you walk away scot-free, something like that?"

"Something like that."

"Why should I?" asked Frank.

Kline shrugged. "I don't know."

"You scratch my back, I scratch yours? That sort of thing?"

"Maybe I'll come in handy someday," said Kline.

"Handy for what? I've been pensioned off. I'm not involved with the force anymore."

"You'll go private," said Kline.

"Don't count on it," said Frank. "Maybe I'll follow in your footsteps and become a criminal."

"Lots of money in the private sector."

Frank grunted. "So, I should maybe let you out on the grounds that if I maybe one day go private you might just maybe come in handy?"

"Sure."

"Too many maybes," said Frank. He reached into his pocket, took out a pack of cigarettes. He lifted the pack to his lips and shook it until he could gum a cigarette out, then tucked the pack away. Kline just waited. Frank fished out a cheap disposable lighter, flicked its wheel until finally he managed a flame. He lit the cigarette, took a drag. "Come in handy how? With that fucking mutilation cult? You wiped them out already."

"Not all."

"No?"

"No."

"Why the hell not?" asked Frank, exasperated.

Kline shrugged. "Not enough gasoline."

Frank shook his head, made a grimace of disgust.

"I'll pay you," said Kline finally.

There was, Kline saw, a different gleam in Frank's eye when he raised his head, a tightness to his mouth. "How much?"

"Twenty thousand."

"Now, where'd you get that kind of money, Kline?"

"Do you really want to know?"

Frank continued idly surveying Kline, the burning cigarette loose in one corner of his mouth, his remaining hand reaching absently over to scratch the terminus of his stump through the denim sleeve.

"No," he finally said.

"You don't want to know? Or you won't do it for twenty?"

"Both," said Frank.

"Twenty-two," said Kline.

Frank shook his head. "Last place you need to be is out loose," he said. "For everybody else's sake."

"Twenty-five," said Kline.

"I'm not saying it's not tempting," said Frank. "But it's cruel of you to wave money around. I'm an honest cop."

"You're no longer a cop, honest or otherwise," said Kline. "You just told me so. Thirty."

"Just to be clear, what we're negotiating is not whether you'll go to prison. You're fucking going. We're negotiating how long you're staying in." For a moment he seemed the old Frank again—confident, in control. "If I walk out of here and give them your real name, you're fucked. Give me one reason why I shouldn't."

"I already told you: maybe I'll come in handy," said Kline.

"Maybe you will, maybe you won't. You better give me a better reason."

Kline hesitated, shrugged. "I don't have one."

They stared at one another for a long time, neither looking away. Finally Frank frowned. "Thirty thousand," he mused. "We do it this way. I don't tell them who you are, but I push them to charge you with all the piddly little shit they've already got on you. You plead, do time. If I need you while you're serving your sentence, I pull a few strings and then come collect you. If I don't, maybe I tell them before your sentence is up who you really are and you go from serving a few years to serving life. How do you like that?"

"Not much," said Kline.

"It's the best offer you'll get," said Frank. "The only offer. You better start liking it. I'll even throw in a name you can give them, something that'll hold up and match your prints once they grow back." He pushed off the bars, peered at Kline. "So, what's it to be?" he asked. "Yes, or no?"

Kline hesitated, finally nodded.

Frank patted his shoulder. "Look at us," he said. "Two broken men, but one of us still has some breaking left to do." He smiled. "Pleasure doing business with you, Mr. Kline, or whatever the hell it is you're calling yourself now," he said. And then he shouted for Dawkes to let him out.

3.

He was processed under the name Werner Haart. Where Frank had come up with the name or what had happened to the man originally connected to it, Kline had no idea. The name came with a doctored fingerprint card, but also with an outstanding warrant on a drug possession charge. *Take it or leave it*, Frank said. He took it.

He gave the name to them and by God the name held. The new man sensed something was wrong, but since he couldn't figure out what and since Kline would be serving time, he let it go. There wasn't much else he could do. Frank turned up in court to identify him, he pled. Six months later, he was serving a five-year term. With good behavior, apparently he might be out in three.

When he was processed he was braced to have someone mess with him over his missing arm, but they left him alone. Apparently he was too beat-up, too scarred, to smell of anything but trouble.

The cell they assigned him had a lock that squealed when you turned the key in it and slid it open. He felt it every single time, gouging its way deeper and deeper into his brain. His cellmate was a petty thief named Barnes. Short, wiry, bad skin, arms thick with blurry tattoos. Serving time for breaking and entering.

"Damn, what happened to your arm?" he asked Kline the first time he saw him.

"Bit it off," claimed Kline. When Barnes kept asking, he throttled him one-armed and held onto his throat until he passed out.

Barnes was quiet for a few days after that. Even later, once the throttling was far enough in the past for him not to feel Kline's fingers around his throat, he never asked Kline questions, but he did talk about himself. There wasn't much to tell: he told the same rambling stories over and over again. Mostly they were about B&Es that had gone right, the loot he'd scored, how smoothly he'd slipped in and out—*like a fucking cat, man, or more like half-monkey, half-cat, the good halves of both, if you know what I mean*. But Barnes always in the end circled back to the break-in that had gone wrong, the one that had landed him in prison.

Soon, Kline stopped hearing him. Mostly he lay on his bunk, staring up at nothing, and tried not to think. He wasn't interested in figuring out where he'd gone wrong. His whole path had been shot through with wrongness, and he was, he felt, lucky to still be alive. If luck was what it was. Most days it felt like misery. Most days, he told himself, he would have been happier dead.

Sometimes, at night, in the darkness, he'd hear the sound of a gun firing. It'd take him a second to realize that no gun was actually firing, that he was just remembering. He could even smell the cordite in his nostrils, feel the soreness in his trigger finger. Whenever that started, he'd get up and pace the cell, hoping to stop the rest of it from surging back. Pacing never stopped it, but he felt a little more capable of facing it if he was restless and in motion. He could keep a step ahead. That was why he'd been drinking, though that was more like two or three steps ahead at first but then quickly no steps at all. Which probably had been why he'd been firing the gun at the blood target—it was a way to keep the dreams at bay. Or maybe not: he could recall cutting himself and smearing the bloody target on the wall, but after that he'd been too drunk to remember anything at all.

One day, the next. One day, the next. All the same day, more or less. Lying on his bunk whispering to himself his fake name, Werner Haart, Werner Haart. At first so that he wouldn't forget to answer when someone called him that, and later hoping that if he said it enough times he'd start to believe it really was his name. Maybe he could stand to be alive if he were someone else. He tried to convince himself that that other name, Kline, belonged to someone else, another person entirely—that whatever this Kline had done had nothing to do with him, with Werner. No, Werner wasn't a killer, the courts had said so. Werner was an addict who had made a few bad choices instead of befriending Bill W.: he was here on a drug possession charge. Werner was still human. Kline, on the other hand, wasn't.

As far as Werner was concerned, Kline was dead. Either Frank would come resurrect him or Frank would forget and he might get out. But once he got out, would he be Werner or Kline? If Kline, what would he do with himself? He'd probably be right back where he started: holed up in a shack in the middle of nowhere, shooting at a target drawn in his own blood, doing a passable job of drinking himself to death. And that, to be honest, was only the best-case scenario.

But for the moment, it was one day, the next, one day, the next, trying to forget who he was, trying to become someone he wasn't, and getting nowhere at all.

4.

He was inside almost two years before they tracked him down. In retrospect, he was surprised it took them that long.

It started simply enough, a man examining him a fraction of a second too long in the shower. Nothing leering or sexual, just a simple glance that stuck too long. Staring first, briefly, at his missing arm and then, longer, at his absent toes. As if the arm had triggered something that the toes confirmed. When Kline looked back, he saw the man was missing three fingers himself. *A three*, he thought at first, and then the man turned and he saw the severed ear. *A four.* A missing toe too. *A five.*

Not a Paul, he thought. The man had the wrong constellation of amputations to be a Paul. At least there was that. The Brotherhood, then. Which, admittedly, was hardly better news.

The same man slowly circled around him through the days that followed until, one day, as if by accident, during mealtime, he came over to sit at Kline's table.

"No," said Kline.

"No?" the man said.

"You can't sit here," said Kline.

The man shrugged and wandered away.

"What was that about?" asked Barnes.

"It doesn't matter," said Kline.

Barnes knew better than to ask twice. They sat eating in silence, slowly. Eventually Kline said, "Who was he?"

Barnes shrugged. "I thought *you* knew," he said. "I thought that's why you turned him away."

"Ask around for me," Kline said.

The man's name was Jacob Orst, Barnes reported a few hours later. It sounded to Kline like part of a surname instead of a whole surname, a name that had had part of itself lopped off. Nobody seemed to know what Orst was in for—some sort of assault, but not the specific circumstances.

Two days later, in the exercise yard, Orst was back. They were trooping around, marching a slow circle. Kline could feel the man just behind him, staring at the back of his head.

"Kline," the man said softly, "Hey, Kline."

Kline ignored this until Orst grabbed his shoulder with his two-fingered hand. "What?" Kline said.

"Hey," Orst said, "I'm talking to you."

"No, you're not," said Kline.

"No?"

"You're talking to someone named Kline," Kline said. "My name's Werner."

"Werner?"

"That's right," said Kline.

"Funny," said Orst. "You look just like someone named Kline."

"That's your problem, not mine," said Kline.

Orst ignored this. "I have a message for you," he said.

"You have a message for Kline," said Kline. "Not me."

"Return to the fold," intoned Orst. "Keep the faith. You belong to us. Come home."

"I already told you, it's not for me."

"Return to the fold," said Orst again, squeezing his shoulder. Then he let go and fell back.

Should have killed him the moment I saw him, Kline thought. *Now it's too late. Now they know.*

He lay on his bunk staring at the bunk above. *Werner Haart,* he thought to himself. *Werner Haart.* He'd been using the name long enough that it was almost like there were two people inside of him now. It was hard not to feel that both were unreal, that both had nothing to do, really, with whoever the hell he really was.

And who is that? some part of him wondered. *Who are you really?*

That was the question. He didn't have an answer, or at least no answer that satisfied him. Maybe he wasn't in a cell after all. Maybe he was still drunk, passed out on the floor of the shack he'd broken into, half dead, half dreaming. If he could get himself to believe that, maybe he wouldn't care about whatever they did to him.

Above him, he could hear Barnes snoring, oblivious.

The Brotherhood wanted him back. They had come asking nicely. If he said yes, maybe they would take him back long enough to kill him. Or maybe, worse, they would welcome him back with open arms.

They would ask nicely once more, maybe twice. Soon, though, they would stop being nice.

5.

He called Frank collect from a prison payphone. "Werner who?" asked Frank at first, and then it clicked. "Oh, yeah," he said, and chuckled. "Fuck. You. What the hell you want?"

"They found me," he said.

"Who?"

"Who do you think?"

"Ah," said Frank. He was silent long enough that Kline worried he'd hung up. "Why tell me?" Frank finally asked.

"I thought you should know."

"Not my problem," said Frank.

"No," said Kline. "It's mine."

"Glad we're agreed on that," said Frank. "You'll have to take care of this one on your own."

"You sure?" asked Kline. "You know how things turned out last time."

"Do what you want," said Frank. "Just make sure nobody's head ends up under my bed."

• • •

Orst was across the prison mess, sitting at a table, watching him, pretending not to be. He continued pretending as Kline strode toward him. At the last moment, when he realized Kline wasn't going to stop, he tried to get up and move away. Kline was faster, his hand falling heavy on the man's shoulder before he was all the way to his feet, forcing him back down.

Once the man was seated again, Kline let go and sat down across from him. Kline could see the panic in Orst's eyes, the way he was primed to flinch.

"You tell them," said Kline. "Tell them that there's no Kline here. Only Werner."

"They already know who you really are," Orst said.

"Werner," Kline repeated. "And even if I were this Kline, judging by the looks of you I'd never come back to their goddamn fold."

"You really want me to tell them that?"

Kline nodded, started to stand.

"You're throwing in with the Pauls, then?" accused Orst.

Kline froze. After a moment, he sat back down. He reached out and laid his hand on top of Orst's hand, very lightly. It was a struggle for Orst not to pull his own hand away.

"I'm not with you, I'm not with the Pauls, I'm not with anybody," Kline said, very softly, voice almost a whisper. "I'm not a joiner. Haven't any of you learned that by now?"

"I don't think you understand—"

"I do understand," said Kline.

"You're telling them to come after you," said Orst.

Kline smiled. "Let them fucking come."

6.

Another week, two. Orst kept his distance now, which was, Kline quickly came to believe, a bad sign. Did he care? He wasn't sure.

Why even fight? He didn't value his life, not really. When he had been found, he'd been drinking himself to death. He was well on the way to becoming something inhuman, and would just as soon have been dead.

But it just was not in his nature to roll over. Maybe that was all it came down to. Perhaps it even *was* his nature, all that remained of it, to fight. Perhaps that will to fight was all he really was now.

Something within him lifted its snout and scented the air. It smelled of blood. It wasn't that he felt any more human, but he did feel alive. More so than he had in a long time.

"Haart," stated the prison guard. "Visitor."

It took him a moment to remember this was his name, that the guard was talking to him, the pretense of his new identity punctured now. "A visitor?" he finally asked.

But the guard had turned and was already shuffling his way to the gates that led to the visitors' room.

Kline followed. *Frank, maybe*, he thought.

He moved through the first gate, waited beside the guard for it to close and the second gate to open. Then it was down the hall and through a propped-open door. He followed the guard to the third table in a line of tables, each cut in two by a pane of heavy plexiglass, a phone receiver embedded in either side of the tabletop. Nobody was on the other side.

He sat down, waited.

He knew who it was before the man arrived, could feel it somehow. Then the man sat down and examined him through the plexiglass. He looked precisely as he always had. The man picked up his phone receiver. After a lengthy hesitation, Kline picked up his own.

"Hello, Mr. Kline," said Gous, his voice echoing slightly and sounding oddly distant through the phone, despite his being only a few feet distant.

"Did you come to thank me?" asked Kline.

Gous gave a half smile. "For what?"

"How many Pauls are left?"

"A half-dozen," said Gous. "You burned most of us. But we'll rebuild."

"You'd have burned too," said Kline, "if you'd been there."

"I'm not going to thank you for that."

"You're welcome," said Kline.

Gous regarded him for a long time. Finally, he said, "I wanted to see with my own eyes that it was you. I wanted to be sure."

"Are the Pauls planning to kill me too?"

Gous shook his head. "We'll leave you alone," said Gous. "But we don't have the numbers to stop the Brotherhood from doing what they want to you."

"I won't join them."

"I'd ask you to join us, but last time you did, you torched the place."

"I don't want to join you either."

Gous nodded, stared at him, considering. "Why are you still alive, Mr. Kline?" he finally asked.

"Who says I'm alive?"

"Ah," said Gous. "Still afflicted with a philosophical bent, I see. Do you think that will do you any good when they come for you?"

"How is it none of you ever learn your lesson?"

"Neither do you, Mr. Kline," said Gous. He regarded Kline for another long moment. "Would you care to give me a reason why I should help you? Maybe you'll be useful to us someday? You have information that might be of help in . . . Fill in the blank. Anything?"

"No, Gous," said Kline.

"Not Gous," said Gous. "Paul."

"It's hard for me to think of you as a Paul," said Kline.

"Why? I'm missing a hand, like all the other Pauls. My hair is blond. I fit right in." He leaned forward. "But I'm not just a Paul," he said. "I'm the new head Paul. I run the place now. The irony of this was that they made me that because you decided to save me. *You* chose me."

Surprised, Kline began to laugh.

"So Ramse is in charge of the Brotherhood and you're the head of the Pauls," he managed to get out.

"Haven't you heard, Mr. Kline? Ramse is gone."

"Gone?"

"As in dead. They killed him."

...

He stared. His cell door was open—it was the time of day when inmates could come and go. He just lay there.

When he had last seen Ramse, the man had assured him he was in a position to assume the leadership of the Brotherhood. According to Gous he had, and then one of the others, a nine, nine amputations, had usurped his place. DeNardo, the name was. He had pushed Ramse out a window, or, rather, had had him pushed. Officially, it was an accident.

At the time, when Ramse told Kline he could take over, Kline had offered to kill DeNardo. He had killed so many people that day that one more wouldn't have mattered. But Ramse had said no, he could handle it. Apparently he'd been wrong. Which was why he was dead.

He had liked Ramse, despite himself. Moreover, he had made an agreement with Ramse. They had had an agreement to leave one another alone. With DeNardo, however, there was no agreement.

There was a noise, a shout, either from the catwalk that ran alongside the cells or from the central space below. He sat up, hesitated. More shouts, the sound of police whistles. By the time he was on his way to the cell door, an alarm was sounding. A second later, all the cell doors slammed electronically shut.

Gripping the bars, he looked out. The noise came from the catwalk. A man spattered in blood, cradling his arm, stumbled toward him. The man's head was covered by a burlap sack, but Kline could tell from the smeary tattoos on his arms that it was Barnes.

He was walking slowly, stumbling, one arm holding the other pressed to his chest. His skin was very pale, except where it was spattered with blood. He clipped the side of the catwalk and lost his balance and tumbled down, and Kline saw that his right hand had been removed, cleanly severed.

He lay there, blood dribbling from his wrist and spreading in a pool beside him, until guards in riot gear arrived in force and dragged him away.

And so we begin, thought Kline.

7.

Three days passed without incident. *Same length of time it took for Christ to rise from the tomb*, he thought, absurdly. He acted the same as usual, only now his movements were more precise, he was more attentive. The world was coming alive for him again, growing richer in color, bloodier. It felt good in the same way that slowly losing your mind feels good.

And then, on the third day, outside, in the yard, the crowds parted a little to either side. On the near side was him and on the far side was Orst. *Red Sea*, he thought, and once he thought this it seemed natural for him to walk down the empty furrow.

Orst had two men flanking him. Both were missing fingers. *Ones,* scoffed Kline, *barely.* He came and stood near them, not threatening, just ready, waiting for Orst to grow nervous and speak first.

It didn't take long.

"Did you get the message?" Orst asked.

"It was misdelivered," Kline said.

"No," said Orst. "We knew what we were doing. We don't want to hurt you, not if we can help it."

"Orst," said Kline, turning the name around on his tongue. "What did it use to be before you became one of them? Horst? Borst? Forster?"

Orst looked confused, maybe a little offended. "It was always Orst," he said.

"I find that hard to believe," said Kline. He turned and walked away.

"What shall I tell them?" called Orst from behind.

Kline turned. "Tell them no."

"No, you didn't get the message?"

"Just no," said Kline, "as in never."

"DeNardo won't take no for an answer," said Orst.

"He'll have to," said Kline. "Tell him this is his last chance. If he keeps it up, I'll kill him."

Barnes spent nearly a week in the hospital ward before being returned to the cell. He looked like a whipped dog. They had not been able to reattach the hand—or rather, said Barnes, they hadn't even bothered trying.

He lifted his stump. "Just like they used to do to thieves in the olden days," he said. His gaze fell to Kline's missing arm. Under his gaze Kline could feel the phantom limb that was not there start to tingle. "Now we match," Barnes said.

"You'll have to lose the rest of your arm before we match," said Kline. "Is that what you want? If so, I'm sure that can be arranged."

"Who did it?" Kline asked him a little later.

"I don't know," said Barnes.

"You don't know?"

He looked like he was going to weep. "They had the sack over my head before I knew what was happening."

Kline nodded. After a while, though he already knew the answer, he asked, "Why?"

Barnes shook his head in despair. "Just before they cut the hand off, one of them whispered into the sack 'Return to the fold.'" He looked at Kline in confusion. "What does that even mean?" he asked. "I've been careful, I haven't gotten in anybody's way. I haven't offended anybody. Return to what fold?"

Kline just shook his head. It was already too late. Barnes knowing that he had been chosen only because he was Kline's cellmate wouldn't help anyone, least of all Barnes.

It took another day before he caught Orst alone. Or not alone exactly. The two other men, the ones with eighteen fingers between them, weren't far away, only a dozen feet or so. But a dozen feet was enough.

He didn't have a weapon. He suspected Orst did, a knife probably, or the equivalent—something sharp, pointy. He momentarily considered trying to take this knife from Orst and using it on him, but it'd take too long to find it, let alone take it away, let alone use it. The two henchmen would be on him well before that.

Instead, before Orst even knew he was there, he grabbed the man's remaining ear and pulled down as hard as he could, simultaneously ramming his forehead up and through Orst's temple.

Almost immediately, Orst was down, semiconscious, confused, his ear torn from his head and still clutched in Kline's hand. Kline's head was shooting with pain from where it had struck Orst's skull.

In a rush, the two henchmen were upon him. They hit him maybe a dozen times, the blows falling hard enough that his hearing started coming in waves. And then, as suddenly as it had begun, the beating stopped.

Orst had risen to one knee and was waving at them. *No, no*, he was saying, or at least that was what Kline thought were the words the man's lips were forming. And then his hearing began to come back.

"Can't you see?" Orst was saying to the pair. "We should be thanking him. He elevated me! He's made me a six now, six amputations. The lost prophet has taken his first steps in his return to the fold!"

What was there to say to that? Disgusted, Kline stumbled up, flicked the ear away, fled.

Orst didn't rat him out, but he still got two days in solitary. He was, after all, covered in blood. On the second day, in the darkness, just as he was getting used to the people he had killed circling around him, was almost ready to start having meaningful conversations with them, a guard released him, took him back to his cell.

The top bunk had been stripped bare. "Where's Barnes?" he asked.

"Haven't you heard?" the guard said. "Barnes is dead."

Of course he hadn't heard. He'd been in fucking solitary.

"How?" Kline asked.

The guard just patted him on the shoulder. "They'll assign someone new to your cell soon," he said. "For now, enjoy the extra room."

...

Orst was back in the general prison population, gauze taped over the hole where his final ear had resided. One of the two henchmen was in solitary, probably under suspicion of Barnes's murder. The other stuck close to Orst.

Kline asked around, but nobody would tell him any details. Finally, a con named Sanchez who ran a smuggling operation said, "He's dead. What does it matter?"

"I want to know how," said Kline.

"Knowing doesn't bring him back."

"Everybody's been told not to tell me," said Kline.

"That's right," said Sanchez. "They don't want it happening to them."

Disgusted, Kline shook his head, turned to leave.

"Not so fast," said Sanchez. "You want information. What have you got to trade?"

"What do you want?"

Sanchez looked at him appraisingly, then frowned. "You don't have anything I want," he said. "But I'm going to tell you as a favor."

"You want me to owe you one."

Sanchez shrugged. "Maybe I just want someone who tears his enemies' ears off to think of me as a friend."

"All right, let's hear it," said Kline.

"Your friend Barnes got Red Queened."

"Red Queened?"

"You know, like *Alice in Wonderland*. 'Off with his head.'"

At night, while he slept, Barnes visited him, carrying his severed head in the crook of his arm. When he spoke, the lips of the head moved, while up above blood welled from the remains of the neck and dripped down his shoulders. His voice came in a low whisper. Kline had to concentrate to hear him.

"Hello Barnes," Kline said each time he showed up.

"They killed me!" Barnes said with a sort of wonder.

"Yes," said Kline. "They did."

"Why didn't you warn me?"

"What good would it have done? No good at all."

"You know what I think?" said Barnes, slowly. "I think you didn't tell me because you didn't want to feel responsible. You wanted to pretend you weren't involved."

Kline did not reply.

"There was no reason for me to die," Barnes said.

"That makes you no different from countless others the world over," said Kline. "And yet they're all dead."

"Not you," said Barnes.

"No," said Kline. "Not me. Not yet."

"When?" said Barnes. "When?"

8.

"Had a change of heart?" asked Orst. He still had only one of his henchmen with him, the other not yet out of solitary. This one was missing two fingers now. He had been elevated. The pair were careful how close they got. They kept the mess table between themselves and Kline.

Kline put his hand on the table, where it would be in plain sight to one side of his tray. He flexed his fingers, waited.

"Well?" Orst finally said, his voice a little tense now. He was irritated, but trying not to show it.

"Who wants to know?"

"You know who."

"No," said Kline. "No change of heart."

Orst shook his head. "Sooner or later DeNardo's going to decide you're not worth it and kill you. Probably sooner."

"Sooner works for me," said Kline.

For a moment, the henchman tightened his fist and Kline thought the man would come at him. If he did, Kline could use the tray. They weren't sturdy, were made to break, but it might slow the man down. After that, his best weapon would be the edge of the table. If he got lucky, he could probably incapacitate the henchman, but whether he could take care of Orst as well depended on how quickly both men reacted.

But after a tense moment the two men exchanged a look and, in unison, moved off.

Final warning, thought Kline.

"I need a gun," he told Sanchez later that day, in the corner of the yard.

"What do you need it for?"

"For Orst," said Kline. "And for the big fucker with him."

"What makes you think I can get a gun?"

Kline just looked at him.

"Even if I could get one," said Sanchez, "you know they'll just keep coming at you. It's not enough just to have one. If I get you one, you have to use it."

"Trust me, I know how to use a gun," said Kline.

Sanchez pretended to think. "Why would I want them dead?" he finally asked. "Why wouldn't I make things easier all around and let them kill you?"

"If you don't want to get me a gun, just say so."

"I'm considering," said Sanchez. "Don't rush me."

Kline let him think. He stared out at the rest of the yard. At a distance, Orst was watching him, his henchman too.

"Why does he hate you so much?" asked Sanchez. "Because you're both missing shit? He feels competitive or something?"

"He doesn't hate me," said Kline. "He's following orders."

"From who?"

"From outside."

"Who does he belong to? The Brand? Brödraskapet?"

"Nothing like that. It's a religion."

"What sort of religion?"

"More like a cult. Amputation based. They think the more you cut off the closer you are to God."

Sanchez swore under his breath. "You used to be part of this?"

Kline shook his head. "They tried to recruit me because I was missing my hand. I said no. They keep trying."

Sanchez fell silent again.

"He's watching us," Kline said. "Orst is."

Sanchez shrugged. "Let him watch. I'm not afraid of him."

"No?"

"No," said Sanchez. "You, though, the jury's still out on." He gestured at Orst and his henchman. "That other one with him had all his fingers until a few weeks ago."

"That's right," said Kline. "You're observant. Orst converted him. The one in solitary too. Now there's less of both of them."

"Fuck me," said Sanchez. "Now they'll do anything Orst says?"

"They'll follow his orders. He's a six."

"A six?"

"Six amputations. In their minds he's exalted."

"I'm not giving you a gun," said Sanchez. "Maybe because I don't have one to spare right now or maybe because I have too many questions about you." He looked at Kline. "Your name isn't Haart. I knew Haart and you're not him. How the fuck you got in here under his name and what you're really up to, God only knows. That makes me nervous. So, no gun. But I'll get you a knife," he said.

"In exchange for what?" asked Kline.

Sanchez shrugged. "I liked the way things were before. We had it balanced out. There's no room for a new group in here, especially not one that's recruiting. Take care of this problem and make it go away."

"I'll take care of the problem," said Kline.

"Unless it takes care of you."

"I'll take care of it," said Kline evenly. "Where do I find this knife?"

By the time he got back to his cell it was waiting for him. It was not a knife exactly, but a makeshift shiv made out of some sort of thick metal strap. One end had been hammered and bent gently around, wrapped over and over with duct tape to form a handle. There was almost no guard between the blade and the handle. He'd have to be careful not to slice open his palm. The other end was filed to a point, both edges ground down fine, sharp and slightly jagged. It looked crude, but the balance was good. The handle was good too, not likely to slip much. And the blade was firm enough neither to bend nor break.

He made a few passes with it, felt how it slid through the air. It almost didn't resist at all when he changed direction. It was a vicious, precious thing, less crude than it looked on first glance.

It was small enough for him to slip between his waistband and his hip without it showing, and the duct tape handle would hold it in place.

He slid the pad of his thumb along the blade, felt the skin catch, watched a thin line of blood appear.

9.

He was deep within his dreams, headless Barnes still there and lugging around his own bloody head, the mutilates he had slaughtered standing gawping in a mute chorus, there to witness his unraveling, when from under his arm Barnes's head said, "What's that?" *I don't hear anything*, he answered, and Barnes answered, "No, not *hear*," and inhaled deeply.

Instantly Kline was awake. There, huddled just outside his door in the twilight of the half-lit catwalk were two shapes. He could smell the mix of aerosol and lubricant they were spraying into the lock to keep the key from squealing.

Who had turned off the mechanism that kept all the cells electronically closed at night? How much darker was it in the cell than in the hall? Enough, he hoped, that they couldn't see him even though he could see them.

As quietly as possible, he slid off the bed and wriggled underneath.

At the doorway, they stopped for a moment, motionless. He watched from beneath the bed, holding his breath while they stayed still, letting it slowly out only once they had started moving again.

Where was the knife? He'd had it under his pillow, within easy reach. He'd left it up there.

He edged toward the head of the bed and worked his hand up between the metal frame and the wall, as quietly as he could. He heard the slight whisper as the cell door slid open, felt the way the light from outside flickered as the pair moved in. He had to force his arm up to get his hand high enough to reach the top of the mattress, and even then he could only get his fingers over to the knuckles. He could feel the edge of the flat pillow but couldn't reach under it far enough to find the knife.

He stretched a little further, the metal of the bedframe cutting into his forearm. This time, when he reached, his fingertips brushed the blade.

He tried to coax it closer, but he couldn't get purchase.

The two men were just beside his bed now. He could see the movement of their legs, hear their breathing. He stretched again, hoping they wouldn't see his fingers, that they were hidden under the pillow. He brushed the knife, but only succeeded in pushing it another half-inch away.

He heard one of the pair inhale deeply and then something hard struck the bed with a thump, making the mattress quiver. Once, twice, and then it stopped.

"Where in hell is he?" he heard one whisper, and then a creak as they straightened to look into the upper bunk. He stretched his own arm up again and there the knife was. In hitting the mattress, they'd bounced it toward him.

He worked his arm back through the gap and lay flat, only then realizing that he'd already cut himself on the blade. He repositioned the knife so he was grabbing the handle.

He watched the legs of the men. When the moment seemed right, he quietly swept the blade out, slashing through the nearest Achilles tendon.

The man it belonged to gave a muffled scream and swayed. Kline heard a thunk and saw a makeshift club of some sort strike the floor. It was already rebounding up. The knife had gotten fouled in the heel of the man's shoe and Kline almost lost his grip on it. His hand ached where he had sliced it open. The man took a half step and then fell, dragging Kline partway out from under the bed.

He wrenched the knife free. Orst, trying to support the other man, had gone partway down with him. Kline, on his back, spun and kicked Orst as hard as he could in the knee, sending a burst of pain through his bare heel. Letting go of the other man, Orst crabwalked backward toward the cell door. Kline lashed out at him and the knife split open the sole of his shoe. The other man was groaning and trying to get hold of Kline, or maybe he was begging for his life, hard to say. Whichever it was, he kept it up until Kline stabbed him in the throat.

The man stopped trying to grab him. Kline could hear him wheezing now where his windpipe had been split. He heard too the sound of him swallowing the blood that was beginning to fill his throat.

"Don't move," Kline told him, voice flat. "I'll be right back."

He stood and, barefoot, made swiftly for the door.

Orst was on the catwalk, still crawling away backward, perhaps in shock. One leg didn't seem to be working as well as the other. *Maybe he'll have to cut it off,* thought Kline, and then thought, *Seven.* When he saw Kline, Orst moaned and spun over, trying to get to his feet, but his leg simply wouldn't support him.

Kline fell on top of him, pressing the knife to his throat.

"Shhh," he whispered into the hole where Orst's ear had been.

Orst went limp. For a moment Kline thought he'd passed out, but no, the man's breathing was too erratic for that.

"What are you going to do to me?" Orst whispered.

"I'm going to kill you," said Kline.

"Please," said Orst, his voice beginning to rise. Kline pushed the blade harder against his throat.

"You think you deserve to live?" Kline asked. "What does that mean, deserve? Shall we ask Barnes?"

"I, I'll leave you alone. I'll tell DeNardo that it wasn't you after all."

"A little late for that."

"I can convince him, I swear."

"You'd betray your faith? Lie to your spiritual leader?"

"I, I don't want to die."

"You mean to tell me you've had six amputations and that's as deep as your faith runs? Tell you what," said Kline. "Renounce the Brotherhood and I'll let you live. Leave the fold, Orst."

"But—"

"Say it," said Kline. He improvised. "I renounce my faith. I curse God. I have been misled by the Brotherhood and I have misled others. I deserve to burn in the fires of hell. I shake the dust from my feet and curse the Brotherhood."

For a long moment Orst was silent, and then Kline pressed the knife further and this time felt it split skin. Trembling, with Kline's prompting, he began to recant his faith. He was crying, though whether out of fear or because of shame over what he was doing or both Kline wasn't sure. No doubt Orst wasn't sure either.

When he had finished, Kline whispered into the hole where the most recent ear had been, "We both know I'm still going to kill you."

"Then why—"

"I just didn't want you to die believing you were going to heaven."

"Get thee behind me, Satan!" Orst said, his voice shaking.

"Satan?" said Kline. "You flatter me."

And then Orst took a deep breath to shout for help and Kline slashed his throat from missing ear to missing ear.

He left the body lying there, the wiped-down knife on the catwalk beside. He stood and stumbled back to his cell. The men in the cells he passed watched him cautiously. He didn't acknowledge them.

Inside the cell, Orst's henchman had crawled partway under the bed. He was lying in a puddle of his own blood. Kline grabbed him by the foot to drag him out and found that he'd not only severed the tendon but slashed through most of the ankle. He couldn't find purchase. He switched to the other foot and dragged the man out that way.

The man was dead or close to it. In any case, he didn't protest as Kline dragged him slowly into the hall and down along the catwalk.

He left the man there, dead or almost dead, beside Orst, then went back into the cell, closed his eyes, and slept.

10.

He was in the middle of a building, a vast empty space. He wasn't sure how the ceiling above him could support itself, the space between walls so vast that he expected the ceiling to sag and collapse. Near one corner was a set of stairs, floating slabs of stone without rail or banister. Twelve steps led up to a large stone slab, a landing, also without rail or banister or wall, which led to another set of steps that went to another slab, and so on, and so on, up to the roof and perhaps beyond.

He started climbing. By the fifth step he had begun to experience an intense vertigo, but despite this he made it to the first platform. He tried not to look over the edge or get too close to it. Whenever he took a step, he could feel the stone beneath his feet shudder. Nevertheless, he forced his way across the platform and to the next set of stairs.

What was supporting them? They seemed to be just hanging there, in open air.

He began again to climb, this time on hands and knees. The sensation of vertigo was almost unbearable. If he looked at anything other than the stair directly in front of him, the world began to spin.

He made it halfway up the flight and wasn't sure he could go further. But it was worse staying there, his face resting on one cold stair, his hands on another, his knees on a third, feeling nothing but empty air between. He managed another stair, then another. But he still hadn't reached the platform when, abruptly, he awoke.

His bed was surrounded by guards in riot gear. Some were brandishing tasers. They were inches away from him, staring.

"Don't move," said one.

"What, morning already?" said Kline. A moment later, his face was being pushed into the floor and what felt like dozens of hands were holding him down.

"Where did you get it?" the warden asked. The shiv was on the man's desk. He kept picking it up and putting it down again.

"One of the two of them brought it," claimed Kline. "They intended to kill me."

"But it didn't work out that way."

"No, it didn't," Kline agreed.

The warden picked up the shiv again, twirling it in his fingers. "The thing I don't understand is why you didn't call the guards."

"I was sleepy," said Kline. And then once it was clear the warden was disinclined to accept this: "Someone gave them the key to my cell and disabled the autolock. If I had called a guard, how would I know I wasn't calling the guard who had arranged for them to get into my cell?"

"Are you saying a guard did this?"

"No. I'm saying a guard helped."

"Any idea who?"

"Any of them missing any fingers?" asked Kline. "No? If not, I'd make them all take off their socks and check that they have all their toes. Anybody missing one or more, I'd mistrust. Then again, maybe it's not a religious thing. Maybe someone just did it for the money."

"I don't think you should go around blaming guards, considering the trouble you're in."

"Me?" said Kline. "I was defending myself. I was minding my business in my cell when Orst and his buddy showed up with a club and a knife. Anybody would have done exactly what I did."

"You expect me to believe you had no weapons, were attacked by two men, and managed to take their weapons away and kill them?"

Kline held up his bandaged hand. "You can see what happened when I made a grab for the knife. I'm lucky to be alive."

The warden shook his head.

"Self-defense," said Kline again. He smiled softly. "The security footage should make that clear." When the warden began to grow uncomfortable, Kline feigned incredulity. "You mean to tell me something went wrong with the footage? There's no recording? Someone sabotaged it? Seems like you're the one in trouble, warden, not me."

There was an inquiry. A guard was quietly let go, though Kline never did find out if he was a member of the Brotherhood or just someone hoping to make a little extra cash. Kline stayed in solitary for two weeks while they stewed over what to do with him. In the end, they simply released him back into the general population, perhaps thinking that someone there might do away with him and solve their problem. Six weeks after that, he was told they had found insufficient evidence of wrongdoing on his part. He would not be charged.

Sanchez congratulated him. Everyone else gave him a wide berth.

"Man, you're a legend now," said Sanchez. "I might have a place for you."

Kline just shook his head.

Sanchez looked at him for a long time, then nodded. "Yeah, sure," he said. "For now."

His dreams were easier, for no reason he could understand. He was no longer visited by the dead. He got a new cellmate and immediately made the man strip down so he could confirm he had all his digits.

"Dude, you paranoid," the man said, a little freaked out. But it wasn't long after that they established a regular and companionable rhythm, neither getting in the other's way.

He had a visitor waiting, he was told. When he went to the visitor's room, he found it was Frank.

The man was wearing a new suit, and had started dyeing what was left of his hair. His cheeks had filled out a little. All in all, he looked younger than he'd looked two years ago, before Kline had started to serve time.

Kline picked up the handset, waited until Frank picked up his.

"Hello, Frank," he said.

"You've been a busy boy, I hear," said Frank.

"Self-defense," Kline said.

"You're not even going to deny you did it?"

"It was them or me," he said.

“The thing I can’t figure out is why every time it’s either them or you it always ends up being them.”

“Just lucky, I guess.”

“I don’t know that luck has anything to do with it. How long until your parole board?”

Kline shrugged. “Three months, maybe four. They haven’t given me a firm date yet.”

“What do you think? Is Werner Haart sufficiently rehabilitated to return to society?”

“You tell me,” said Kline.

“No,” said Frank, “absolutely not.”

Kline’s jaw tightened. “You planning to block my parole? Keep me locked in here a few more years?”

“I wish it was that easy,” said Frank. “No, just the opposite. I’m going to bump your hearing up. Someone has found a use for you.”

PART TWO

1.

They brought him a paper sack containing his possessions, led him to a room where he could change. His clothing had been laundered, pressed, and packed away right after he was sentenced: once he put them on, the creases were clearly visible and didn't fall out. Other than clothes, there was a key on a keychain that read *Sunshine State*. The key he recognized as his former apartment key, but he wasn't the sort of person who would ever have owned that keychain.

That was all: one set of clothing, a key to an apartment he no longer owned, a keychain lauding a state he'd never visited.

When he exited the changing room they led him to the inner gate and opened it for him. He stepped through and waited until the gate closed behind him. Then he waited some more. He was between the gates for long enough that he had begun to wonder if the outer gate would ever open. When, suddenly, it did.

He walked out. The outer gate clanged shut behind him.

He waited in front of the prison a while. Not having a watch, he couldn't be sure how long. Nobody came.

He started walking.

...

A car drove past him, heading toward the prison, then another. He kept trudging on. The third car that passed spun a U-turn, came back to creep alongside him. An early-50s Pontiac Chieftain Catalina, white hardtop roof, forest-green body. It might have qualified as vintage if the body hadn't been spattered with rust. Kline bent down and peered in.

"Get in," Frank said.

Kline clambered in. Frank was driving before the door was fully closed.

"Didn't think you were coming," said Kline. "Thought maybe you forgot."

"I didn't figure it'd hurt you any to cool your heels and wait. Only you didn't wait."

Kline didn't bother to respond. The sun was coming strong through the dusty windshield, catching on the glass in strange ways. He squinted against it. In prison, he had never had enough sun; now he suddenly had too much. No matter which way he turned his head he couldn't escape it. He closed his eyes, but still sensed it flickering through his eyelids.

"You're not falling asleep, are you?" asked Frank.

"No," said Kline.

"Good," said Frank. "We have things to discuss."

"A lot has changed since you went inside," said Frank. "Things have happened."

"Things are always happening," said Kline.

Frank glanced over, face creased with mild disgust, then looked back at the road. "You always were an asshole," he said. "You should be nice to me. I just got you out of prison."

"The way I remember it, you made sure I spent time in prison."

"I could have done nothing at all and then your fingerprints would have grown back and they'd have figured out who you really were. You'd be dead now. On death row, anyway."

"What do you want?"

"*I* don't want anything," said Frank. "I'm just the delivery boy, transporting you to where you're wanted."

"Where's that?"

Frank shrugged.

They kept driving, the road straight, the sun bright. Kline's head had begun to ache dully. He let Frank's evasion stand as long as he could bear. "Where?" he finally asked.

"Where?" asked Frank. He leaned toward Kline and offered a grotesque smile. "That would be telling."

The sun, the motion of the car around him, made him feel ill. It was a struggle to remain still. Frank kept glancing over at him, then glancing away. The man seemed to be enjoying himself.

They came to the freeway and got on, headed south. They drove for some while in silence.

Eventually, after about an hour, things started looking familiar. Kline began to get nervous.

"Where are you taking me?" he asked.

Ignoring him, Frank turned on the radio. He held the steering wheel steady with his knee and twisted the tuning knob with his remaining hand, trying to find reception. Eventually, he settled for an oldies station. It kept fading in and out. After a few moments, he switched it off again.

"There are other stations," said Kline.

Frank just grunted. When he signaled to get off the freeway, Kline recognized the exit.

"Frank . . ." Kline warned.

"Just relax," said Frank.

"Where the fuck are you taking me?"

"No need to get worked up."

They curved around the cloverleaf, Kline feeling the thud of blood low in his ears. About halfway through the arc, he reached over and grabbed the steering wheel.

"What the hell are you doing?" shouted Frank.

Kline didn't answer. Just tugged.

The car veered toward the shoulder and the slope beyond. When Frank tried to tug the wheel back, Kline twisted and struck him hard in the ribs with his knee.

Frank gave a bellow of pain and crumpled toward the wheel. Kline drove his forehead into Frank's temple, shoving Frank's head against the driver's side window. The car tires zipped as they crossed into the rumble strip, and then the car tipped, the wheels on Kline's side leaving the road. Then the other wheels left the road too and the car was briefly level again before it began to drift down the slope.

Frank was shouting, trying to push him away. Kline ground his head into his temple, trying peripherally to keep an eye on the descent. For a brief moment the car felt like it was going to roll, but then Kline wrenched the wheel just enough to prevent it. He shouted for Frank to brake and the man did, and there they were, in dirt and sagebrush, Frank's hand leaving the steering wheel and groping for Kline's throat, unable to get his hand properly positioned as long as Kline kept his body pressed against him. Kline felt Frank's hand touch his arm and wander up it, looking for something it could throttle, but before it could get anywhere at all Kline had removed his own hand from the steering wheel and tightened it around Frank's windpipe, cutting off his breath.

Frank's face was a blur because of its proximity, but Kline watched what he could see of it. It was going slowly red and thick, the lips shivering as the man gulped for air.

"Where are we going, Frank?" Kline hissed in the man's ear.

He loosened his grip slightly and Frank took a deep juddering breath.

"You crazy bastard," he sputtered. "Are you trying to kill us both?"

"No," said Kline. "Just you," and he tightened his grip again.

Once Frank was unconscious, there was a moment when Kline found it very hard to loosen his grip. It was, he thought later, as if his fingers knew something he did not. How much easier would things have been for him had he simply killed the man then and walked away?

There was nothing to prevent him from killing Frank. And yet he didn't kill him. His false name, Werner, asserted itself in his mind, and the humanity he once had had flexed and tingled like a phantom limb until the real fingers on his remaining hand opened and slackened and let Frank live.

By the time Frank had regained consciousness, Kline had pawed a gun out of the glove box. He held it pointed vaguely in Frank's direction.

Frank groaned.

"Welcome back to the land of the living," said Kline.

"You're still here," said Frank. "I hoped it was all a bad dream."

"Maybe it is. Where are you taking me?"

"To your new boss."

"Give me a name, Frank," said Kline.

Frank shrugged. "You would have found out soon enough anyway. I'm taking you to Paul."

"Paul? Gous, you mean."

Frank nodded. "If you like. Used to be called that."

"Why? To kill me?"

"Kill you?" Frank looked surprised. "Why would he want to do that?"

"What, then?"

"He has a job for you."

"A job? Don't you remember how all this started when the Brotherhood had a job for me?"

"Just hear him out. You can do that much."

"Why you?" asked Kline. "Why would Gous hire you instead of simply sending a Paul?"

"He didn't hire me," said Frank, not meeting his eyes.

Kline felt a vague dread begin to rise, like bile. "He didn't?"

"No," said Frank. "He didn't have to." He patted his empty sleeve. "He sent a Paul. You're looking at him."

He was probably twenty yards from the car before Frank or Paul or whatever the fuck he chose to call himself now started yelling.

"Kline," he yelled. "Kline! Come back!"

He did not come back. He kept running, stumbling down what was left of the slope until it flattened out.

"You can't run, Kline!" yelled Frank. "They'll find you! Not the Pauls, the others! The Brotherhood! They'll find you and kill you!"

Kline ignored him, kept running. He squeezed through a gap in a chain-link fence. A moment later he was crossing a gravel lot.

In another hundred yards he awkwardly climbed a lower fence, dropped down onto a stretch of cracked sidewalk. He slowed to a walk, catching his breath.

He considered. He had no money. He could pawn Frank's gun, make a little that way, enough to buy a bus ticket out of this god-forsaken town anyway. He would go . . . where? Somewhere else. And from there, somewhere else. Maybe find that deserted shack again, set about drinking himself to death, this time in earnest. But he'd want to keep Frank's gun if he did that. After all, if he went back to the shack, he already had a target to shoot at.

He stopped walking. It was absurd.

Then he shook his head, started walking again.

He walked another six blocks before the Pontiac pulled up along-side him and stayed there, rumbling.

"Can I have my gun back?" asked Frank.

"No," said Kline.

"You know I can report you on a parole violation for carrying a firearm, don't you?"

"Report me."

"Don't be like this," Frank whined. "Come on, get back in the car."

"A Paul?" said Kline. "How the hell did that happen?"

"I was as surprised as you," said Frank. "What do they say about God? That he shows up when you're least expecting him? Besides, they're not like the Brotherhood. They're different. More sensible."

"That's one word for it," said Kline.

"They took me in," said Frank, ignoring him. "Gave me a job. Your idea of me going private was a decent one. Only problem was nobody wants to hire a one-armed ex-cop when there are more than plenty two-armed ones to go around. Paul took me in."

Kline didn't say anything, just kept walking.

"Come on," said Frank. "What else are you going to do?"

What else *was* he going to do?

"Paul needs you," said Frank.

"I don't know any Paul."

"Gous, if you insist on calling him that. Gous needs you. Someone has been slaughtering Pauls. He needs your help."

"Doesn't he remember what happened last time I helped?"

"He remembers," said Frank. "But that first investigation was a setup, not real. This one is real. He also knows you know how to take care of yourself."

"This crime is real?"

"Oh yes," said Frank. "Very much so. We'll show you the bodies right away. What we have of them."

"What do you mean, *What we have of them?*"

"Come find out."

Kline just stared.

"Come on," Frank wheedled, "get in the goddamn car. What can it hurt?"

"What's the crime?" asked Kline.

"Come and see," said Frank.

Kline shook his head. "Don't make me strangle you again."

"You're no fun," Frank said. "Never were."

"What's the crime," repeated Kline.

"Mutilation," said Frank.

Kline laughed. "That's not a crime for them. *If thy right hand offend thee*, and all that. It's a way of life."

"Murder first," said Frank. "They were murdered and then were mutilated afterward."

"You should have led with murder," said Kline.

"Which is the greater crime?" asked Frank. "Murdering someone or desecrating their corpse?"

"Is that a trick question? Murder, of course. Always murder."

"Wrong," said Frank. "Wrong, wrong, wrong. Killing someone is a crime against them. Desecrating their corpse is a crime against God."

Kline rolled his eyes. "Every time I think I have you bastards figured out you come up with some new nonsense. Nobody cares what happens to a corpse, God least of all."

Frank didn't rise to the bait. "Are you getting in or not?" he asked.

"I'm not," said Kline.

Then, with a sigh, he opened the door and climbed in.

2.

On the way, they passed the place where the headquarters of the Pauls had been before Kline burned it down. Where the building had once stood was now only an empty rectangular hole. The only sign left of the conflagration was the scorch marks on the bricks of the buildings to either side.

"They didn't rebuild?" asked Kline.

"The fire damaged it badly enough we couldn't get permits to renovate. We had to tear it down."

Kline just grunted. They drove a block or two in silence.

"Proud of yourself?" asked Frank.

"Not particularly," said Kline.

They turned off the street and into a suburban neighborhood. Frank drove slowly down a meandering avenue before abruptly turning onto a smaller road. Soon, they came to a wrought-iron gate about twelve feet high. When the car neared, the gate jerked once, then slid smoothly open.

On the other side was a guard shack and a barrier arm. A guard leaned out of the window, squinting. When Frank waved to him he gave a slight nod, opened the barrier arm. He nodded again to them as they went through.

They drove slowly down a winding road, passing a series of houses, each possessed of just enough property and trees to stay hidden from its neighbors.

"All these houses belong to the Pauls?" asked Kline.

Frank shook his head. "Just one. Otherwise, it's a run-of-the-mill elitist gated community."

"What do the neighbors think of you?"

Frank shrugged. "Everybody keeps to themselves here."

They turned onto a single lane road. They passed three driveways on one side, four on the other, before coming to a mailbox reading *P. Paul.* Frank pulled into the driveway just beyond it.

"What does the P stand for?" asked Kline.

"What P?"

"In P. Paul."

"For Paul."

"As in Paul Paul?"

"Exactly," said Frank.

The driveway was made of what Kline initially thought were white pebbles but which proved to be crushed shells. At the end was a house, not exactly small but more modest than Kline had anticipated, far from a mansion. Gous was standing on the front porch. He came down the stone steps and hovered near the car, waiting. As they got out, he held his hand out to Kline.

"Ah, Mr. Kline," said Gous. "I'm glad you're here."

Kline reluctantly lifted his own hand. Gous awkwardly pressed Kline's hand once with his remaining digits and then without a word turned and headed inside. Kline and Frank exchanged a glance, then followed.

• • •

They moved through a parquet entry and up a staircase. At the top was a carpeted hallway with a pair of double doors on one wall. They passed through them and into what must originally have been a bedroom but had now been converted into an office.

A set of locked filing cabinets lined the wall to the right. Gous took a seat in the center of the room, behind what Kline recognized to be the former chief Paul's desk. He gestured Kline to a chair on the other side. The desk's surface had been sanded and refinished, but the legs and sides had been left as they were, blackened by fire. To Kline, the desk still smelled vaguely of smoke. Perhaps he was just imagining it, like someone suffering a stroke. On the wall behind Gous were the two paintings from the office in the old headquarters. Or at least Kline assumed they were the same paintings: the surface of each was blackened and cracked, the images all but gone.

"Nice place," said Kline, sitting. "Though a bit smaller than the last one."

"There are fewer of us. It's sufficient, for now."

"For now?"

Gous nodded. "We will return home once we have the means to rebuild."

"Why not stay here?"

"This is not the chosen place," he said, as if explaining to a child.

Kline didn't know what to say in response.

"Mr. Kline," said Gous. "I don't want to irritate you, but I must ask. How do you feel about what you did to us? About the wrath you brought down? About the desecration of our sacred place? Do you have any regrets?"

"Regrets?" said Kline. "Why would I?"

"Do you truly mean that?" Gous asked. "Do you have so little concern for the lives of others? Would you prefer it if I were among the dead?"

He opened the desk drawer and extracted a pistol, placed the barrel's snout against the side of his head.

"Well, Mr. Kline? Shall I pull the trigger? I believe in you. If you tell me I should, I will."

"I—" Kline started, and then closed his mouth. He was suddenly reluctant to speak. He did not want to be implicated in Gous's death but, even more than this, he did not want to be tasked with saving the man either. Gous waited with one eyebrow raised for him to shake his head or nod. Kline did neither.

"Ah, uncertainty," said Gous. He lowered the gun, replaced it in the desk drawer. "The great doubter, always. Why must you insist on taking the most difficult path, Mr. Kline? Do you think it will make all the difference? What difference could that possibly be?"

"Did you bring me here to try to convert me?"

Gous smiled. "You've already been converted, Mr. Kline. You just don't realize it yet."

"No," said Kline. "I haven't."

Gous shook his head sadly. He gestured to Frank, who stood near the door. "Look at Paul there," Gous said, "with his remaining arm and hand hanging awkwardly on one side of him, mercifully empty air on the other. Even he eventually opened his heart and let us in."

"Amen," said Frank, in a tone that struck Kline as tinged with irony.

"But not you, Mr. Kline," said Gous. "Never you."

"Just tell me why I'm here," said Kline.

"In a moment," said Gous. "Patience is a virtue." He splayed his remaining fingers, took a deep breath. "Paul was right about you," he said. "The first Paul, our founder, I mean. He really was. There is something special about you, even if you willfully close your eyes to it." Gous stood and walked slowly around the desk, came very close to Kline. He squinted a little. "And yet he was wrong, too," said Gous. "He thought you were the prophet, the Messiah come at last. But that was never your role, was it?" Gous cocked his head. "Quite the opposite," he said. "You were, rather, God's exterminating angel, come to cleanse the world with fire."

Kline's missing arm began to tingle, to ache.

"Mr. Kline, we were hard of hearing. We had stoppered our ears against you. Making us understand who you truly were took extreme measures." Gous made a slight bow. "I thank you for taking them," he said. "We all do."

Out of the corner of his eye, Kline saw Frank bowing as well. "You're thanking me for incinerating you," Kline said flatly.

"If that is how you choose to interpret it," said Gous.

"What other way is there?" Kline turned to Frank. "I thought you said the Pauls were the less crazy ones."

"Shut up, Kline," said Frank. "Pay heed to Paul."

"Yes," said Gous. "Pay heed to Paul. To me. Will you reconsider, Mr. Kline? Will you cease to be lukewarm? Will you cease to pursue the whirling banner hither and thither and instead cast your lot with the righteous?"

"I have no idea what the hell you're talking about," said Kline.

"You sadden me, Mr. Kline, both you and your unwillingness to see what is right before your eyes."

"Back to where we started. Gous, I have nothing against you," said Kline steadily. "I might even be just a little grateful to you for getting me out of jail. That remains to be seen. But let's get on with it."

"Why?" asked Frank, voice cutting. "Late for an appointment with drinking yourself to death?"

"Paul . . ." warned Gous.

"You were living like you wanted to die," said Frank. "And yet you never attempted to take your own life. Why not?"

"Paul!" said Gous sharply. "Leave us."

Frank hesitated, then, mouth a taut line, he turned and went.

Gous slowly made his way back to his own side of the desk. And yet he did not sit down. Instead, he stood there, hand gripping the chair's back. *Now that Frank's gone he's keeping the desk between us*, Kline realized. *He is afraid of me.*

"I understand your impatience, Mr. Kline," claimed Gous. "But I must beg your indulgence. It won't take long." He gestured to the door. "Please, follow me. There's something you must see."

Gous led him out of the makeshift office. Frank was waiting just outside the door and, at a gesture from Gous, fell into step beside them.

Gous led them downstairs and deeper into the house. "Someone has been butchering us," he told Kline over his shoulder. "For a long time, we thought it was probably one of them."

"One of who?"

"The Brotherhood. But they claim to have nothing to do with it."

"Some of their own people have been killed too," said Frank.

Gous nodded. "And their own people have been desecrated in the same way as ours."

They arrived at a swinging door. Gous pushed it open with his stump, and they passed through into what proved to be an entirely ordinary kitchen. It was empty, the counters as immaculately clean as would be the case in a model home: a carefully arranged knife block full of knives that looked like they had never been used, a perfectly folded tea towel, nothing else visible. Kline wondered if there was anything in the cabinets.

"Where are the other Pauls?" asked Kline.

"I thought it would be better if it was just us for now," said Gous.

They passed through the kitchen and crossed a breakfast nook, coming to a door. Gous rested the remains of his hand on the handle, stopped.

"Of course," he said, "it could still be the Brotherhood. Someone in authority could deliberately be thinning their own ranks as well as our own for their own obscure purposes."

"But you don't think so," said Kline.

"No."

Kline turned to Frank, eyebrow raised.

"I don't either," said Frank. "It doesn't feel right."

"It's not their style," said Gous. "This is new."

"New how?"

Gous smiled faintly. "Better if you see for yourself."

"How many bodies are we talking about?"

Gous shrugged. "Not that many by your standards. Four that we know of. Three of ours and one of theirs. There may be more of theirs. If so, our spy inside the Brotherhood hasn't managed to get us word yet."

Gous depressed the handle and opened the door. On the other side was an unfinished garage, smelling of concrete dust. The garage was empty except for a large upright industrial freezer humming against the far wall. The handles of the doors had been wrapped with a chain and padlocked shut. "It wasn't cheap," said Gous. "The freezer, I mean. It probably set reconstruction of the temple that you burned back some. But it seemed a necessary expenditure."

He turned to Kline, a key extended in his hand. "Go ahead. Open it," he said.

"Why me?"

Gous looked at him. "Do you think this is a trap, Kline? That we sprung you from jail and brought you here so that we could get rid of you in some arcane way? If we wanted to kill you, Paul would have done it already."

"Still happy to oblige," mumbled Frank under his breath.

Kline ignored him. "What's inside?" he asked.

"Open it and see," said Gous.

Kline turned to judge the distance between himself and the door, found Frank had a pistol out now.

"Where did that come from?" Kline asked.

"I want my other gun back," said Frank. "Also, do as Paul says."

"Yes," said Gous. "Heed Paul. Me."

Kline's mouth had gone dry. He slowly reached the gun out of his pocket and handed it to Frank, who took it and handed the first gun to Gous. Gous awkwardly slipped it into his pocket, then extended the key again to Kline.

Kline reached out and took hold of the key, jiggled it into the lock. He rotated it and the padlock popped open. Unhooking it from the chain, he let it drop with a clink to the floor. He listened to see whether Frank or Gous would move to pick it up, if that would give him a chance to take Frank's gun. Neither did.

He unwound the chain from the handle, letting it drip link by link to form a little heap at his feet. And then he tugged open the freezer door.

A rush of cold air and frost, a mist of sorts rising up and almost immediately dispersing to reveal the corpse of a man, naked. Something wrong about it: seen from the side, hanging, a meathook running into its back, just below the scapula, not deep enough to go all the way through, just deep enough to hold it, swaying, upright. Its toes brushed back and forth along the floor. And then the body swung a little and he realized, suddenly, what it was that was wrong.

"Jesus," he said, amazed.

He threw the other door open and saw two more bodies, similarly positioned, both male, one clothed, one not, possessed of various amputations. He leaned into the freezer, felt the cold enter his throat as he moved. He coughed. He reached out and touched the first body and turned it on the hook, only to realize things were even worse than he had originally divined.

"Why the hell did you hang them?" he asked, not taking his eyes off the corpse.

"They came with the meathooks attached," said Gous. "They must have been hanging somewhere before they were sent to us. We thought the hooks might be important for you to look at. A clue."

Kline turned the body further until it was facing toward him, as if regarding him. It had been cut exactly in half, bilaterally, the bridge of the nose split perfectly down the middle. He could see the brainstem, half the throat, the inner workings of the spine, the carefully bisected penis.

"Where's the other half?" he asked. "In another freezer?"

"We don't know," said Gous. "This is the only half we've been given."

"It must have been frozen solid before they cut it," said Kline. "Otherwise impossible to cut it so evenly."

"I thought so too," said Frank.

Kline's hands were aching, both the hand that was there and the hand that was not. He tried to move them and the hand that wasn't there moved easily. The other had become stuck to the frozen body. He tore it away, and after a moment dots of blood welled to the surface of his palm. He wiped them off on his pants, tried to ignore the stinging. It wasn't hard: he'd had a fair amount of practice.

He came close again, this time not touching the body.

"It's perfectly cut," he said. "Meticulously done."

"It almost sounds like you admire it," said Frank.

"Paul," said Gous, warningly. Then to Kline, "This is the best one. The most perfectly preserved. The only one we received before it had begun to thaw. I'm not surprised you were drawn to it."

"What's that supposed to mean?"

"Shall we say that you are possessed of a spiritually discerning temperament, Mr. Kline?"

Kline grunted. It was hard for him not to touch the body again. He felt like his missing hand was still touching it. "Bandsaw maybe," he said, as he closed the freezer doors. His hand left a bloody palm print on the steel exterior.

"Yes," said Gous. "Likely."

"Meatpacking plant. Somewhere with both huge freezers and tools to cut through meat and bone."

"Perhaps," said Gous. "Frank investigated every meatpacking facility within driving distance, but didn't find anything."

"Could be just a grocery store meat department with a walk-in freezer and one good bandsaw," said Frank. "I looked into plenty of those too, but a little hard to say it's any one of them unless you catch someone in the act. Could even be someone with an elaborate home setup. An industrial grade table saw that they've modified, put a larger blade on."

Kline turned to Gous. "You've got Frank looking into this," he said. "You don't need me."

"We do need you."

"Why?"

"Because Paul hasn't managed to solve it."

"Paul?"

Gous pointed at Frank. "Paul."

"Frank, you mean. He at least handled homicides back when he was a detective," said Kline. "I didn't. If he can't solve it, I can't either."

"I have faith in you, Mr. Kline," said Gous. "I have seen you do the impossible."

"And if I say no?"

"We put you back in jail," said Frank. "This time under your real name. For good."

Gous frowned. "No need for threats, Paul," he said. He turned back to Kline. "If you say no, you say no. We will cross that bridge if we come to it."

"How is that not a threat?" asked Kline.

Gous just smiled softly.

"And if I try to solve the crime and fail?"

"We will cross that bridge too if we come to it," said Gous.

For a long while, Kline was silent. "If you lie to me," said Kline finally, "if I find—ever find—that you've lied to me, faked some aspect of the crime, kept some salient detail hidden from me, misdirected me, whatever, I will come back and slaughter both of you."

"We understand that you are capable of this," conceded Gous.

"I work the case for three days," said Kline. "I'll solve it if I can. If I don't, then I walk away. No repercussions."

"Think again," said Frank.

"Three days, and then we talk," said Gous. "Reevaluate."

"No," said Kline. "Take it or leave it. Kill me now if you don't care for the deal. According to Frank, I'm just going to drink myself to death anyway."

"Aren't you?" asked Frank.

Gous bowed his head, closed his eyes. Frank, Kline saw, immediately imitated him, although, squinting, he kept his pistol trained on Kline.

"Dear Lord," prayed Gous. "We are gathered here today, thy servants, to ask for guidance in the fulfillment of thy will."

"Stop it," said Kline.

"Thy reluctant servant, Kline," Gous prayed, raising his voice, "demands a term for his service, a term of the same length it was decreed would pass before thy Only Begotten Son would arise from the darkness of the tomb. May we grant to him this boon, asking of Thee that Thou shalt either see fit to soften his heart before the sun sets on the evening of the third day or give us the guidance needed to bring this matter to a swift conclusion?"

"Stop it!" shouted Kline.

"Amen," said Gous, and opened his eyes.

"Amen," echoed Frank.

"What's the matter, Kline?" asked Gous. "Afraid you might begin to believe?"

"No chance of that," muttered Kline.

"No," said Gous. "Because you believe already. The risk is that you will admit so to yourself." Gous smiled gently. "I have had my answer from God, Mr. Kline. You may have your three days and then you shall go free, unmolested." He turned to Frank. "Paul, you shall accompany Mr. Kline and assist him."

"What?" said Frank, startled.

"Like hell," said Kline.

"To keep you honest," said Gous to Kline. "To ensure that you try. It has been written. He shall be with you, Mr. Kline, whether you wish it or no. He shall be your so-called right-hand man. This, I am afraid, is nonnegotiable."

3.

He sat on a stool at the island of the immaculate, unused kitchen with Frank sitting on a stool across from him, never quite able to stop hearing the hum of the industrial freezer coming muted through the garage door.

"Here we are," said Kline.

"Trust me, I don't like it any better than you do," said Frank. "Stop wasting time reminiscing. Let's solve this fucking thing so we can go our separate ways."

"Any ideas?" asked Kline.

"I'm pretty sure it's a case of murder," said Frank dryly.

"Who's wasting time now?" asked Kline. He folded in on himself, stared at the countertop. His days as a detective felt several lifetimes away. He tried to summon that former self up, suddenly saw again the face of the man with the cleaver, the first man he had killed, out of necessity. He was surprised that that face was in his head still, that it hadn't been crowded out by all the others he had killed since.

"You didn't get anywhere trying to figure out where he's cutting up the bodies," said Kline. "Too many possibilities."

"Yes," said Frank.

"Then I won't get anywhere that way either. You don't think it's someone in the Brotherhood. Or the Brotherhood as a whole doing it. But you're not absolutely certain."

Frank nodded.

"Hard to investigate the Brotherhood in any case. Gous has his spy over there looking into it," said Kline. "Maybe that spy is enough."

"Paul."

"Of course the spy's name is Paul," said Kline. "He's a fucking Paul."

"No, the other," said Frank. "Our leader. His name is Paul, not Gous."

"Potato potahto," said Kline. "How about the other Pauls?"

Frank shook his head. "There are only six or seven remaining. I'm as sure as I can be that it's none of them."

"But it could be."

Frank shrugged. "It's not."

"You're sure you're not blinded by your faith?"

Frank hesitated a moment, seemed actually to be seriously considering the question. He finally shook his head. "Fuck you," he said, "but no."

"Who does that leave?" asked Kline.

"You tell me."

"Anyone disgruntled who left the Pauls?"

"Not since I arrived."

"We ask Gous about that," said Kline. "Doesn't have to be recent. Family of someone who died in the fire might be a possibility as well. Or anyone with a grudge against the Pauls."

"Or against the Brotherhood."

"Or against the Brotherhood. Someone who was in one and then in the other maybe, then left altogether. Or . . ."

Frank just waited. Kline had a faraway look. After a moment, he shook his head.

"Or what?" Frank said. "Finish the thought."

"I was just thinking," said Kline. "What if it's not one person? What if it's a whole hidden sect? What if there's been another schism?"

4.

“No,” said Gous. “Not possible. We’d know.”

“Any Pauls you lost in the fire whose bodies remain unaccounted for?”

“I—” said Gous, and then stopped. “No,” he said, but he dragged the word out for too long. “There may . . . have been one or two Pauls we presumed dead who just used the fire as an . . . occasion to leave. I don’t think so, but it’s not impossible.”

“I want the names of anyone presumed dead whose bodies weren’t actually found,” said Kline. “Along with anything we can use to track them down if they’re still alive.”

“What about Paul?” Frank asked Gous.

“Their names before they were named Paul, I mean,” said Kline. “Telling us Paul, Paul, and Paul were presumed dead but may in fact still be alive isn’t going to get us anywhere.”

“No, no,” said Frank. “This one was named Paul before.”

“But he was found,” said Gous. “We know he’s alive.”

“But he left the Pauls?” said Kline. “You’re telling me that somebody named Paul left the Pauls?”

"He was gravely injured," said Gous. "He leaped from a window to save himself from the fire. Misjudged and landed on a spiked wrought-iron fence. Broke his back. Punctured a lung. Paralyzed from the waist down."

"There," said Kline. "That's something."

"You think a paraplegic has been committing these murders?"

"Not him," said Kline. "But maybe someone pissed off about what happened to him."

They came up with five people. One was a woman Gous remembered as having been kicked out of the Brotherhood early on, but he wasn't quite sure of her name. They also had Paul, the paraplegic. There was one other who had survived the conflagration with severe burns but whose mind had boiled and bubbled with the heat so that he had been released from the hospital straight into a mental ward. And then two others, presumed dead in the blaze, whose bodies had never been found.

"Probably because they burnt up," said Frank.

"Probably," said Kline. "But we check, just in case."

It took some time for Gous to dredge up a possible name for the woman. When Kline tried to look her up in the phone book, he couldn't find her.

"You sure that's the name?" said Kline. "Madrevida?"

"Madrevida's right. Or close at least," said Gous. "But I can't remember the first name at all. Something starting with a vowel."

"Maybe she changed her last name," said Frank.

"Was the Brotherhood pursuing her?" asked Kline.

"No," said Gous. "They kicked her out. Excommunicated her. She didn't want to leave."

"Why was she excommunicated?" asked Kline.

"Is that important?" asked Gous.

"It might be," said Kline.

"She . . . objected to one of the Brotherhood's methods of making money."

"The calendars?" guessed Kline, remembering the stacks of calendars he had seen in the Brotherhood, each new month showing a nude woman with one more amputation than the last.

"What calendars?" asked Frank.

"Yes," said Gous, ignoring him. "She was one of the early months. She criticized the decisions of those who were closer to God than she. Soon, she was gone."

"What was she?"

"A four, I believe. So, April. One major amputation, the others minor: a hand, three toes."

"You don't recall her first name?"

"I hardly knew her," said Gous. "Just her last name. Madrevida. Or Malavida, maybe. You think she could be our problem?"

Kline shrugged. "How can you find her exact name?"

Gous sighed. He picked up the phone.

Gous dialed a number and then turned on the speakerphone. They listened to the phone ring. Frank, Kline saw, had grown alert, was sitting abnormally still. Gous was doing his best to look at ease, but was far from successful.

"What's wrong?" asked Kline.

"Shut up," said Frank. "Don't say a word."

The line was picked up, but whoever was on the other end didn't say anything. They listened to the crackle of it for perhaps a dozen seconds.

"Yes?" a voice finally whispered.

"Is that you?" Gous began.

"No," said the voice, no longer a whisper, and Kline watched the blood drain from Gous's face. "The individual you are trying to reach can't come to the phone on account of being deceased. I imagine you know why. Would you care to know how?"

"No," said Gous. "Please don't."

"I was wondering if you'd call," said the voice. "Was it to explain to me what you're doing with Mr. Kline?"

"What makes you think we have Mr.—"

"I am always a step ahead of you, Paul. Always. You had your little fun with your spy for a while, but only because I let you have it. Please put Mr. Kline on the line."

"He's already on," said Gous.

This seemed momentarily to surprise the voice. At least it hesitated before speaking further.

"Mr. Kline, are you there?"

"I'm here," said Kline.

"We've met before," claimed the voice. "Years ago, back in the bar in the Brotherhood, back before you decided to go on your little killing spree. You were the first self-cauterizer I had ever met, a real inspiration. You were, at the time, very drunk."

"If you say so," said Kline. "And you are?"

"What? You can't guess? I'm DeNardo."

"The one who murdered Ramse," said Kline.

"I didn't murder him," said DeNardo. "I had him murdered. Would you care to hear how?"

"Not particularly."

"Of course you wouldn't. It's yesterday's news. You're a man who lives in the present, not the past. Mr. Kline, I want to make the offer again, but this time with my own mouth so you can hear how sincere I am." He cleared his throat. "Mr. Kline, you have made a grave error casting your lot with the Pauls. I want to give you the opportunity to correct this error. Leave the Pauls. Cast your lot with me."

"I haven't cast my lot with the Pauls," said Kline.

"You must pardon me for doubting you, Mr. Kline. That you are to be found among them suggests otherwise."

Kline didn't say anything.

"Come back to the fold, Mr. Kline," said DeNardo.

"What are you? An eleven? Twelve?" asked Kline.

"A thirteen," said DeNardo, proudly. "Ear, ear, nose—"

Kline cut him off. "Then why are you demeaning yourself by talking to me?"

"Demeaning?" He sounded hurt. "No, no. You are . . . special, Mr. Kline. I acknowledge that certain among us cannot be judged by their amputations alone. There is something . . . more to you."

Kline was silent.

"Paul?" said DeNardo.

"I'm here," said Gous.

"I have a head to return to you. Kline might appreciate that particular gesture having made it himself a time or two. Certainly I thought of him when I decided to sever your man's head. And the nerve of you—spying on us with a member of our own sect of guards! I had to take care of it myself: if I'd informed the other guards there would have been a trial, a whole enclave, a general mess. The guards feel like they're in charge of their own. But if someone simply disappears, well . . . Don't send anyone else to infiltrate us. If you do, next time I will come for all of you. Kline?"

"What?"

"I ask you again, will you return to the fold?"

For a moment Kline didn't say anything, and then he offered, "Is Madrevida still with you?"

"Who? Malagrida, you mean?" said DeNardo, suddenly off-balance. "I didn't realize you knew her. She's been gone from here a long time."

"Are we talking about the same person? What was her first name?"

"Angelique?"

Kline glanced at Gous, who nodded.

"That's the one," said Kline.

"If it's important to you, if it'll make a difference to your decision, I can see about finding her. She hasn't been with us since—"

Kline reached across the table and disconnected the phone.

When, a moment later, it began ringing, nobody answered.

5.

Frank got a buddy still on the force to run Angelique Malagrida's name through the system. All that came up was a driver's license. She had hair dyed jet black, pale skin, eyes so dark brown as to seem black. They had the name of the mental facility that Paul, formerly known as Douglas Blevins, was housed in. They found the address of the parents of the paraplegic Paul, as well as the former addresses for the two Pauls presumed dead.

"Which first?" asked Frank, buckling his seatbelt. Gous stood at the front door, face expressionless, looking lost.

"The presumed dead first," said Kline. "Then the paraplegic. After that, we'll see."

They drove. In the rearview mirror, Kline watched Gous watching them leave. By the time Kline lost sight of him, he still had made no move to go back inside the house.

"Is Gous all right?" asked Kline.

Frank shrugged. "He has three bodies in his freezer. What do you think?"

"One and a half bodies," corrected Kline.

Frank laughed. "Have it your way," he said. "Three half-bodies, let's say. That might not bother someone like you, used to lugging heads around. But it bothers the rest of us."

"Give it time," said Kline. "You'll catch up."

The mother of the first of the presumed dead claimed not to have seen her son in several years. She still seemed distraught, and she clutched a wadded tissue in one bony hand as they spoke.

"We had a falling out," she claimed.

"Over what, ma'am?" asked Frank.

She reached out and touched Frank's empty sleeve. "Over that," she said. "He felt wrong. He claimed he had been meant to be born in a body with only one arm."

"Ah," said Frank.

"Did you feel that way too?" asked the mother, suddenly vaguely hopeful. "Can you explain it to me?"

They made their excuses and got out of there. They didn't inform her that her son was almost certainly dead. They just fled.

The second had not been living with his parents when he joined the Brotherhood, but with a girlfriend, a hard-bitten chain-smoker who, as soon as she saw they were amputees, slammed the door in their faces and threatened to call the police.

Frank knocked on the door. "We just want to talk, miss," he said. "We don't want to hurt you."

"I won't talk to you!" she yelled. "I don't want to end up like Johnny!"

"Is Johnny there?" asked Kline. "Is he with you?"

"What the hell are you talking about?" she said. "He's with you!"

Frank turned to Kline. "Good enough?" he asked.

Kline nodded. "Probably dead. Mark him off for now. If nothing else pans out, we'll come back and apply a little pressure."

The paraplegic had been in residence in an assisted living facilty once he'd gotten out of the hospital. He had been there, the resident nurse told them, for quite some time, and then, fairly recently, his sister had come to pick him up.

"Do you have an address for the sister?" asked Kline.

"Of course we do," the nurse said, "but I'm not allowed to give that sort of information out."

"No?" asked Frank.

"I'm afraid not," said the nurse.

Frank turned to Kline. "You want to handle this or should I?"

"Be my guest," said Kline.

Frank turned back to the nurse. "I have twenty bucks that says you will."

The nurse offered a smile at once cold and apologetic. "It's against regulations," he said.

"How about this," said Frank, getting out his wallet. "I put this twenty on the counter and then I don't worry about what happens to it. It belongs to whoever picks it up. Meantime you get up to use the bathroom but leave that file in your hands on the desk before you go."

The nurse shook his head. When he reached for the phone, Frank batted his hand away.

"Looks like we've got ourselves a zealot," he said to Kline.

"Takes one to know one," said Kline.

The nurse was out of the chair and had backed against the wall. He glanced toward the half door that served as an exit from the space behind the counter. Kline drifted slowly toward it, cutting off that avenue of escape.

"Just relax," Frank was saying. He was patting the air with his lone hand. "Nothing to worry about."

"Here's how this is going to work," said Kline. "In the end, we're going to look at that file. The easy way is for you to let us. Nobody gets hurt. Nobody ever has to know. Nobody gets in trouble. Maybe you make fifty dollars."

"What happened to twenty?" asked Frank.

"Inflation," said Kline.

"What's the hard way?" the nurse asked.

"The hard way is to slit your throat and then look at the file anyway."

"We don't have to kill him," said Frank. "We could just maim him. Lop off an arm, maybe."

"If we just maim him, he can identify us."

"What if we blind him?"

Kline thought for a moment, shook his head. "No, he's heard our voices. Easier all around if we just kill him." And then he corrected, "Well, easier for everybody but him, anyway."

The nurse began to whine.

"Easier still if he lets us look. Then nobody has to die. So what's it going to be?" asked Kline, turning back to the nurse. "The easy way or the hard way?"

"You wouldn't have killed him," said Frank as they drove away.

"You don't think so?"

"No point to it," said Frank. "You threaten him a little and sure, he might call the police, but they wouldn't come after you hard, not for that. You murder him, they're after you until they find you."

"You're smarter than you look," said Kline. "And definitely smarter than that nurse."

They stopped for gas.

"You want to pump or call Paul?" asked Frank.

"Why do we need to call Gous?"

"To keep him abreast," said Frank. "He's the boss. And to make sure he didn't remember someone else."

Kline walked over to the payphone, inserted some quarters, dialed. Gous picked up immediately. "Yes?" he said. "What is it?" He sounded anxious.

"Nothing's wrong," said Kline. "Just checking in."

He explained what they had already done.

"Good," said Gous, "That's two off the list. Who's next?"

"We went to see Paul the paraplegic but he's no longer in the facility. We're heading to his sister's place now."

"His what?" said Gous.

"His sister," said Kline.

"That's impossible."

"What are you talking about?"

"He doesn't have a sister."

"Are you sure?" asked Kline.

"Completely sure."

"Maybe a half sister?" asked Kline. "A stepsister? Something like that?"

"No," said Gous. "When he got out of the hospital we tried to find family to take him in. He doesn't have any."

"Who, then?"

"Could be perfectly innocent," said Gous. "A distant cousin, say, who decided it was easier to pretend to be his sister. Or a girlfriend."

"Or someone the Brotherhood sent."

"Yes, could be," said Gous.

"Or someone connected to your butcher," said Kline.

"Anything's possible."

Kline hung up, walked over to fill Frank in. Frank listened carefully, face grave. "Could be nothing," he finally said.

"Could be," said Kline.

"But I don't like it," said Frank.

"Neither do I."

They drove past the address listed in the file, at normal speed. A half block later, Frank pulled the car over, turned to Kline.

"What do you think?"

"Ordinary house," said Kline. "Lawn's a little long, paint's faded, but otherwise nothing special."

"We knock at the front door?"

"One of us does," said Kline. "Let's have someone around the back too."

Frank nodded. "Go down the alley and figure a way into the backyard and get to the back door. When I ring the bell, count five and kick the door in."

"Will I hear the bell?"

Frank shrugged. "I'll knock too, just in case."

Kline nodded. "I need a weapon," he said.

"A weapon."

"Just in case," said Kline. "How about handing over that gun you were flashing around earlier?"

"The one you took from me and I had to take back? There's only the one gun," said Frank. "It stays with me."

"Why didn't you bring a second gun?"

Frank shrugged.

"You won't be able to use it from the porch," said Kline. "People would see. Bystanders, neighbors. If I'm going in the back, I should have it."

Frank shook his head. "I've seen what happens when you get hold of a gun," he said. "But let me see what I can do."

They got out of the car. Frank popped the trunk and raised the lid. The lug wrench rested on top of the spare.

"You can have that," said Frank.

Kline shook his head. Two crossed metal rods too big and awkward to hide. He searched around for something else, found a torque wrench small enough to slip up his sleeve. Not much, but better than nothing.

When he raised his arm to close the trunk, he felt the torque wrench slide down his forearm toward his elbow then fall back to nuzzle its head against his wrist when he brought the lid sharply down. *Good*, he thought.

He turned and trudged toward the corner. Behind him, he heard Frank's door slam and then, a moment later, the tires crunching against gravel as the car began to move.

He turned right and walked down until, mid-block, he came to an alley. He hurried down it, head bowed, hand in his pocket, trying not to look conspicuous. He passed the backs of yards that had been fenced off, some by chain link that he could see the yards through, others by high wooden fences.

A brick garage, detached, almost fifty feet behind its house, redwood fence to either side of it. An unseen dog striking against an overlapped slat fence, snarling in warning. There: a glimpse of the pale yellow house he'd been looking for. A wooden featheredge fence, just a little taller than him: hard to scale with one arm. The edge of the gate was protruding slightly. *Warped board*, he thought, but grabbed the handle anyway. It was locked, but when he pulled on the gate it popped open.

He examined the latch, saw it had been bent so as not to fully close. Maybe this had happened by accident, but it hadn't happened long ago: where the black enamel was chipped away, the exposed metal hadn't yet begun to rust.

He slipped through, letting the gate swing gently shut behind him. He stayed just inside the fence, examining the yard. Ordinary enough: a stone path leading to a set of concrete steps and a back door. No lawn back here: an ornamental garden of sorts, though overrun and unmanicured, mostly dead.

There was a window to one side of the door, obscured by a white curtain. No lights on inside. He climbed the steps, examined the door closely. Flimsy, no deadbolt, not particularly secure. He listened for Frank's knock, readying himself to kick the door in. And then, on impulse, he reached out and grasped the knob.

Unlocked.

He opened the door as quietly as possible, slipped in.

It was dark inside. He was in a mudroom. Shaking his arm, he coaxed the torque wrench into his hand. He swung it once, adjusted his grip a little. Ahead of him was a kitchen, each of its windows draped with a gauzy white curtain. He quietly pushed the door closed, stood listening.

A low humming from a nearby room, an appliance maybe. No television. No human noise as far as he could tell. He moved into the kitchen (there was the humming, louder now, a refrigerator) and through it, his shoes sticking slightly to the old linoleum. On his way across, he placed the torque wrench on the counter and slid a butcher's knife out of the knife block.

On the other side of the kitchen was a long hallway. He moved slowly down it. He peered through a half-opened doorway, saw an empty bedroom, bedclothes mussed. He went all the way in to make sure it was really empty. It was. He continued on, passing another door, this one shut, then backtracked and eased it open. Another bedroom, as empty as the first, a door in the back corner leading to a bathroom, also empty. He returned to the hallway, heard the doorbell ring, followed by a loud knock.

He froze, held his breath, listening to see if anyone in the house would make their presence known. All he heard was the beating of blood in his own ears and the humming from the kitchen. Moving again, he entered the living room.

The front door opened.

"Hello," said Frank, his voice loud and jovial. "The door was unlocked. Anybody home?"

He poked his head in, saw Kline.

"Empty," Kline said.

"Lived in?"

"Maybe," said Kline. "One bed's unmade at least, and there's not much dust. But nobody's been here for a few days."

"Where the hell are they?"

Kline shrugged. He set the knife down on the coffee table.

"What's that humming?"

"The refrigerator," Kline said.

"A little loud, isn't it?"

For a moment the two men just stared at one another, then Kline scooped up the knife and Frank drew his pistol and together they hurried into the kitchen.

...

The refrigerator had been modified, the partition separating the freezer compartment from the refrigerated compartment below having been cut smoothly out to make a single compartment. The cooling unit for the refrigerator had been turned as cold as it could go, the freezing unit as well. The crisper drawers had been removed. The walls inside were slick with ice.

Inside, crammed in, bent slightly, was a body. Or, rather, half a body, very neatly bisected. It was covered in frost, partly stuck to the back wall.

"Is it him?" asked Kline.

"The paraplegic?" Frank leaned into the freezer, brushed the frost off the half-face. "Yes, probably. Gous would know. He's just like the others."

"Not quite," said Kline.

"No? Because they had to fold him?"

"No hook in his back," said Kline. He struck the body's shoulder with the flat of his palm until the hold of the ice loosened and the body came unstuck from the back wall. He turned it slightly. "See?" he said. "Never was a hook. No hole."

Frank nodded. "Something else too, I think," said Frank. "Can't quite put my finger on it."

They stared at the body. Yes, Kline felt, Frank was right. Something was different. Not just that it had been crammed in. What? He envisioned the other bodies hanging swaying in the industrial freezer, and suddenly he knew.

"It's the other half," he said. "The left, not the right."

"We're back," said Kline.

The nurse's head jerked up. When he saw who it was, his face crumpled.

"Please don't," the nurse said.

"We need a little more information," said Frank, grinning like a shark. "Nothing to worry about."

"You were so helpful the first time we thought it best to come directly to you. A few questions and we'll be out of your hair," said Kline. "You'll never have to see us again."

"I don't know anything," said the nurse. "Please, leave me alone."

Kline ignored this. "The woman who picked him up, his so-called sister, what did she look like?"

"Did she look like him?" asked Frank.

The nurse stuttered, then shook his head.

"Well?" said Frank, his voice sharp.

"I don't, I'm not . . ."

"Calm down," said Kline, his voice soothing. "Take a deep breath and start over. What was her hair like?"

"Long," the man managed.

"What color?"

"Black. Maybe dark brown."

"Good," said Kline. "Thin or fat or somewhere in between?"

"In between," said the man. "Closer to thin."

"See, it's not so hard," said Kline.

"She was pale," the nurse further volunteered. "She was wearing gloves."

"Didn't it strike you as strange that she wore gloves?" asked Frank.

"That's why I remember her," the nurse said.

"Did he call her anything? Say her name?"

The nurse's brow knitted. "Something," he said. "Something a little strange. Angel, he called her once, but that wasn't the strange one. He called her something else too."

"Short for Angelique," said Kline to Frank. "Angelique Malagrida."

"That's it," the nurse said. "Grida."

. . .

They found a payphone and tried to call Gous. No answer. Frank called his contact in the police and had him look up Malagrida again. The address from her driver's license was different from the one she had given the assisted care center.

They drove toward the address, in silence.

"What are you thinking?" Frank finally asked.

"You won't like it," said Kline.

"Probably not."

"It looks more and more like a schism," said Kline.

"Too stealthy," said Frank. "If it was a schism, Paul would know, have some inkling at least. Or, if not Paul, DeNardo."

"The only reason the Brotherhood knew about the Pauls is because they saw the schism occur. It happened publicly. What if a handful of people who were kicked out or simply left later decided to band together? And then, instead of recruiting from the Brotherhood or the Pauls, just approached others as they departed? If they handled it very carefully, nobody would know."

"Nobody's that careful," said Frank.

They drove a little longer, pondering.

"How do we handle this one?" Frank finally said. "Same as the other?"

"No," said Kline. "No ringing the bell, no messing around, no warning. Straight through the front door as quick as we can."

"I'm still not giving you my gun," said Frank.

Kline opened his mouth, closed it again. If he decided he needed Frank's gun, he told himself, he would simply take it.

6.

He was out of the car before Frank had even stopped, stumbling across the lawn and nearly falling, regaining his balance, the car door not quite latching and swinging fully open again as Frank threw the car into park, leaving its back end still jutting into the road. Frank left his own door open as he hustled after Kline, engine still on, the pinging of the door ajar warning sounding behind.

Kline reached the front door well before Frank. He kicked it hard. The door groaned but didn't give, pain shooting back up his leg. He took half a step back, braced himself, and kicked again.

The lock stile split and the door broke through its frame. Frank was right there beside him, trying to shoulder his way past, but Kline pushed in first, skittering on the polished tile floor of the entrance hall and nearly going down. "Police!" Frank yelled from behind him. Kline fleetingly wondered if Frank had forgotten he was no longer police or if it was simply habit or if he just thought it would prevent them from being immediately shot.

Frank was beside him now, gun out and cocked. He touched the barrel to his lips like it was a finger, and Kline understood this to be a sign to be quiet. They both held still, listening.

Nothing.

They crept into a living room, neatly arranged, modern furniture. A kitchen, a bowl of blackening bananas on the counter, a dish drainer full of long-dry dishes. The attached garage was empty, an oil spot on the floor dusted with cat litter, old boxes stacked precariously along one wall. A chest freezer lay near a door that led into the backyard, the baskets belonging to it stacked just to one side.

Kline moved toward it, Frank following. It had a locking mechanism, but when he tugged on the handle it proved to be unlocked. The lid opened smoothly.

It was empty inside, except for a thick rime of frost and two bags of frozen vegetables iced to its floor, one torn, a scattering of blanched freezer-burned peas spilling out.

"Any sign a body was there?" asked Frank.

Kline shook his head. The ice was dirty but showed no sign of blood or other bodily fluids, nor any strands of hair. "That would have been too easy," he said.

"Maybe she's not behind it," said Frank.

"She took him," said Kline. "We know that from the nurse."

"She did," assented Frank. "But maybe they took him from her. Maybe they used her."

"*Who* used her?" asked Kline.

Frank shrugged.

"And where is she?" asked Kline.

"Maybe upstairs," said Frank. "Dead."

The stairs were carpeted; it was easy to keep quiet. On the way through the kitchen, Kline had exchanged his butcher's knife for a long, thin boning blade with a sharp curved tip. He held it in front of him as he went, wondering if it was balanced enough to throw. Probably not.

They reached the top landing, carpeted as well. To the right was a bathroom, empty, a little frosted window too small to crawl out of set in one wall. To the left were two doors, then a third at the very end of the hall.

The first door proved a closet, full of shelves stacked with towels and linens. Nowhere for a human to hide. The second was a home office. A filing cabinet stood with its doors open, empty. There was a desk and a chair, and on the dusty desktop a dustless rectangle where some object had been.

The final door opened into a bedroom. The bed was made, covered by an off-white comforter trimmed with eyelet lace. A closet was hung with women's clothing, a chest of drawers with a stuffed bear on it contained a half-drawer of socks, a half-drawer of panties, a drawer of T-shirts, and a drawer full of silken lingerie.

They relaxed a little.

"Is she coming back?" asked Frank.

"She didn't take much," Kline said. "She'll probably come back to get the rest."

"If she can," said Frank.

"If she can," agreed Kline.

"What now? Wait here or go check out this institutionalized Douglas Blevins?"

Kline opened his mouth to speak when, downstairs, a phone began to ring.

They hurried down the stairs and toward the sound. It came from an old corded phone on the kitchen wall, made of faded yellow plastic. They stared at it. It rang six times, then stopped.

Kline's mind began to spin.

"Keep an eye on the doors," he told Frank. "They may be coming."

The other man took his gun out of his jacket pocket and lumbered toward the front door. Kline kept expecting it to burst open, but it didn't. He took two steps back so that he could see the back door. He held his breath, waited.

Nothing happened.

After a while, Frank went outside and quickly moved the car. Kline looked for alarms or trip wires, but couldn't find any. By that time, Frank was back.

"I parked a block away," he said. "We can get there quickly if we need to. But she won't immediately see it if she comes back."

"She'll notice the door," said Kline. "She'll know someone is here or has been."

"Nothing we can do about that."

Kline nodded. "What are the chances she knows we're here?"

"That call could have been from anyone," said Frank.

"If she doesn't know we're here, she might come back and we might be able to surprise her."

"If she's able to come back."

"If she's able," agreed Kline. "If she knows we're here, either Grida doesn't come back at all, or she comes prepared, maybe armed. Either way, we're in trouble."

Frank nodded. "There's another possibility we're ignoring."

"What's that?"

"That she's dead and somebody else is using this house as a trap."

"Who?"

"It could be anybody," said Frank. "That's the problem. We don't have a fucking clue who might be coming for us."

• • •

The phone began to ring again. Kline froze, fighting the urge to turn his face from the back door and look at it, still expecting someone to come in through one of the doors. Nobody did. It rang, once again, six times, and stopped. He risked a glance at Frank and saw Frank looking back at him rather than at the front door. His face was pale.

"What now?" Frank said quietly.

Kline just shook his head.

It was beginning to grow dark outside. Maybe they, whoever they were, were waiting for dark.

How long had he been standing there? He wasn't sure. Probably just a few minutes, but it felt much longer. He stared at the back door's knob. Perhaps if he gazed at it attentively enough, he would see it begin to turn, regardless of how cautious whoever was on the other side was. At least until it grew too dark to see.

"We should leave," said Frank, speaking louder this time.

Kline shook his head and Frank lapsed back into silence. Frank was, he knew, right. But was it safe to leave now? Wasn't it already too late?

The phone began ringing a third time.

"Maybe you should answer it," said Frank.

Kline shook his head. He counted the rings. One. Two. Three. Frank began to speak again and Kline shushed him. Four. Five. Six. Then it stopped.

Three calls. Six rings each time. Six six six. The mark of the beast.

"We might learn something if we answer," Frank was saying.

"They know we're here," said Kline evenly. "It's a trap. We have to go."

"But—"

"Explain to me exactly where the car is." Kline said. Frank did. "You go out the front, I'll take the back. Try not to get killed. I'll go first. I'll circle around. Count to one hundred. If you haven't heard shots or shouts, you come too."

He stayed low, knife out but held close to his side where it wouldn't immediately be seen. He darted out the door and down the steps, then circled the house, staying crouched and low. Nobody shot at him, nobody was there. He passed to the side yard, came to a chain-link fence about three feet high, a gate in it near the house's wall. He dropped the knife over, opened the latch and passed through, retrieving the knife and blocking the gate with his foot to stop it from clanging shut. He eased it the rest of the way closed and continued on.

Low bushes edging Grida's house. He considered crawling between them and the wall, but if someone was watching him he'd be all the more trapped.

Instead, he slid into the neighbor's yard and crawled onto their front porch, then straightened up and pretended to have just come out of their door. He walked casually down the steps and toward the car in the neighbor's driveway, head bowed slightly, trying surreptitiously to see if there was anyone out there watching him.

Nobody he could see. Either there was nobody or they were very good indeed. He reached the door of the neighbor's car and tried the handle. It was, unbelievably, unlocked. He opened the door and ducked, pretending to get in, falling to his knees instead just outside the car. It was, he hoped, dark enough to fool them.

He pushed the car door closed and crawled rapidly to the end of the driveway.

Then he was up in a crouch and running, taking cover behind the first car on the street.

But someone was already there.

A large man, on one knee, almost a giant. He did not seem surprised to see Kline. As soon as Kline rounded the car, the giant slapped the knife out of his hand. It went skittering down the street. Kline turned to run but the man had him by the wrist and tugged hard enough to nearly dislocate his arm. The man stood and pulled him against his body and wrapped his arms around him and began to crush him. One of the giant's arms felt odd against his back and Kline realized it was because there was not enough arm there: the hand and part of the forearm were missing. The giant couldn't lock hands, which was probably the only thing keeping Kline's ribs from breaking.

"You are Kline, yes?" the giant hissed as he squeezed. "No?"

"I can't . . ." Kline managed, and the man slackened his grip just enough to let Kline take a breath to answer. Instead, Kline screamed.

Frank burst through the front door, shouting. The giant turned, holding Kline before him like a shield, and Frank cursed. The giant shrugged Kline up until his own head and upper body were mostly shielded by Kline's body, his lower body protected by the car. He kept Kline positioned between himself and Frank's gun.

"He can't shoot me," said the giant. His voice was a hoarse whisper, something wrong with it. "Not without shooting you too."

"Then he'll just shoot me too," said Kline.

"This is not what has been prophesied," said the giant.

Frank was edging closer. "Put him down!" he shouted.

Almost soundlessly, the giant laughed. He let Frank come near to the other side of the car's hood, then whispered to Kline, "Tell this Paul to stop or I break you."

"Frank," said Kline. "You need to—"

But Frank cut him off. "I heard him," he said. "It was loud enough."

"Put the gun down on the ground," whispered the giant.

"No," said Frank.

"Or I break him."

"I'm not putting the gun down," said Frank. "And if you break him, I'll shoot you."

The giant grunted.

"We have a standoff," said Frank. "Let's figure a way out of it."

Kline felt the giant shift his grip a little.

"I'll take a few steps back," said Frank, "then I'll point my gun in the air. You take a few steps back as well and then you put Kline down. I'll let you—"

But he didn't manage to finish. The giant suddenly thrust Kline away hard, propelling him across the car hood. For a brief moment Frank lifted his pistol and Kline thought the man might actually shoot him. Then Frank readied himself to catch him, then changed his mind, tried too late to dodge out of the way. Their bodies collided, falling in a heap.

Frank was shouting, struggling, and Kline, breath knocked out of him, was trying to roll free. They flailed, tangled, and then Kline was free and panting and crouching and Frank was on his hand and knees crawling, searching for his dropped gun. At last he found it. He slid up against the side of the car, cautiously poked his head over the hood.

"Where the hell is he?" Frank whispered. Kline shook his head.

Frank stood for a better look. From half a block away, a crash.

Frank ran toward it.

Kline pulled himself to his feet and, limping, set off after him.

He caught up to Frank standing before a shattered fence, a whole eight-foot section of it knocked down. From beyond in the darkness came the yelp of a frightened dog.

The porch light of the house the fence belonged to came on. Kline and Frank darted away.

"We'll go down both ends of the alley," said Frank. "Corner him."

But when they met in the alley's middle, the giant was nowhere to be seen.

7.

They sat in the car, catching their breath, until they heard sirens. Then Frank threw the car into gear, drove.

"Paul will know what to do," said Frank.

"What if he doesn't?"

"He will," said Frank.

But when they reached the house of P. Paul, it was dark. No sign of life.

"Where's he gone?" asked Kline.

"Strange," said Frank. "He's always there."

They sat, listening to the ticking of the engine, considering. Then Frank drew his pistol and got out of the car.

They looked in every room, moving systematically through the house. No sign of anyone, but no sign that anything was wrong either. The rooms were tidy, the beds made, all the clothing still neatly folded in the drawers.

"Where did he send the others?" asked Kline.

"He never said," said Frank. "But wherever they went, they should have been back by now."

It was nearly nine. Eventually Frank holstered his pistol. They waited in the house until a quarter past, but nobody came. In the end, they walked back to the car.

Kline was just reaching for his door handle when a thought crossed his mind. He turned and loped back toward the house.

"What's wrong?" asked Frank.

"Just need to check one thing," Kline said. "I'll be right back."

He opened the door to the garage. He went down the steps. The chains were still off the freezer, which continued to hum busily against the far wall.

He walked to it, placed his hand on the leftmost handle, pulled the door open.

Even before the air cleared, he saw that the bodies inside were packed more tightly together. They had to be, because there was an additional body.

He stared at Gous's profile for some time. He reached out, intending to turn it so as to examine the cut, and then realized that, no, he didn't want to see.

Frank was sitting in the car, his hand on the wheel, waiting. Kline opened the door, sat down beside him.

"Gous is dead," Kline said.

"I know," said Frank.

"You know?"

"She told me," said Frank, and his eyes flicked up to the rearview mirror, his hand still not letting go of the wheel.

Kline turned. Behind them, low in the back seat, holding a pistol, was a woman. Long dark hair, nearly black eyes, pale skin.

When she smiled, only the left half of her face moved. The right half remained paralyzed.

"Hello, Kline," she said. Her voice was a little blurry, slightly deformed, but richer and lower than he'd expected. She smiled. "I'm Angelique Malagrida. But you can call me Grida. I understand you've been looking for me."

PART THREE

1.

He tried to watch her out of the corner of his eye, but every time he even slightly turned his head she waved the gun at him and made him turn back around. She was careful, smart, sitting back far enough that there was no way to grab her or the gun.

"No, Kline," she said, patiently. "Eyes forward." And when she saw him trying to watch her in the side mirror, she made him reach across his body and tip it up so all that it showed him was the sky.

"Better this way," she said. "Now I see you but you don't see me, which frankly is how it's been all along." She gave a strange, tittering laugh. "Even the name, the Brotherhood, tells me you don't pay much heed to people like me, people who are not brothers, people who are not men. You profit from us, exploit us, but hardly see us."

"We're not from the Brotherhood," said Frank.

"Of course not," said Grida smoothly. "You're a Paul. Does that make it better somehow? Tell me, Paul, where is Paula? What about Paulette? Or Pauline?"

"We have female members," said Frank, defensive.

"You call them Paul as well, no? Make them honorary men?"

"Yes, but—"

"Ah, patriarchy," said Grida. "So long in charge they no longer know what they're in charge of. Did it never occur to you that we might have something special to offer, something of which you remain ignorant?"

Frank said nothing.

"Well," said Grida, "you're lucky. I'm going to instruct you. I will enlighten you." She offered that same tittering laugh. Kline found it unnerving, but hoped this didn't show in his face. "One of you, anyway," she said. "That is, if I don't decide to kill you both first."

"You won't kill us," said Frank.

"No? Taken a peek in your freezer lately?" She sighed. "I have no trouble killing those who need killing. So stubborn, so blind." Her voice changed, became harder, flatter. "Now drive," she said.

They pulled out of the driveway, rolled slowly through the gated community and toward the outer gate. At the exit, another car was stopped, brake lights glowing. Someone getting directions, perhaps, or just chatting with the guard. They pulled up behind, idling. This might be, Kline realized, one of their few chances.

"Easy now," whispered Grida, as if she could read his thoughts.

Up ahead, leaning out of his shack, the guard was looking back at them now, still talking to whoever was in the stopped car. Then he turned fully back to the other car's driver and waved goodbye.

The car ahead moved away. Frank rolled slowly forward. When they reached the guard shack Frank stopped, began to crank down the window.

The guard bent toward them.

Before the window was even a quarter down, Grida fired. Frank's window shattered, glass spitting everywhere. The guard's eye disappeared, along with a certain amount of the back of his head. Slowly his body tipped through the window and struck the side of the car, sliding down it, getting wedged between it and the wall of the shack. Frank was yelling something but Kline, deafened by the shot, couldn't make out what. Behind him, Grida was shouting back. And then sound slowly phased back in and Kline could hear again.

"Why?" Frank was shouting. "He had done nothing. There was no reason to kill him!"

"You could have just waved and driven through without stopping," Grida said. "You were looking for the right moment to alert him. It's your fault he's dead."

Frank, angry, shook his head. He tried to look over the edge of the window and down at the guard's body.

"Oh, for heaven's sake, just drive over him," said Grida, irritated. "He's beyond caring what is done to his body." And then, "Kline, kindly remove your hand from the door handle. As you saw, I have exceptionally good aim."

Kline slowly removed his hand from the handle, returned it to his lap.

"Now please reach over and push down the stem to lock your door," said Grida. "Slowly."

Kline did so.

"Very good," said Grida. "There's a chance we're going to get along after all. Drive, Frank. Now."

Frank drove calmly, neither too fast nor too slow. He seemed relaxed, almost placid, except for the way his eye, the one Kline could see, was desperately twitching. In his mind, Kline kept hearing the sound the tires made passing over the guard's body, the lift and thump of the first tire coming over the man's arm, and then the body becoming stuck under the chassis and dragging with a shushing sound beneath the car until finally they turned into the street and that was enough to shake it loose and allow the rear tire to lift and thump, harder this time, over it. As they turned, Kline could see in Frank's side mirror a dark swath that must have been blood, and the dark mound that was what was left of the guard.

They drove for a while in silence.

"There's probably blood all over the side of the fucking car," said Frank.

"Don't be such a baby," said Grida. "It's too dark for anyone to know for certain what it is."

Frank grunted, kept driving, the wind whistling in through the broken window. As the streetlights flashed in and out of the car, his eye continued to twitch.

"Where are we going?" asked Kline.

"Somewhere safe," said Grida's voice from behind.

"Safe for who?" asked Frank.

"And where would that be?" asked Kline.

Grida didn't bother to answer either question. They drove on, Grida occasionally offering directions from the back seat. They passed through the suburbs, circling the edge of town, and then headed west and into the outskirts. Empty lots scattered with warehouses, bottling plants, factories. The road here was deserted, other cars infrequent. They started across a one-lane bridge. Halfway over, they saw a police car on the other side, just under the streetlight, waiting its turn to cross.

"Don't look over at him," said Grida. "Everything is fine."

But Kline couldn't help but cut his eyes over even as he kept his head facing straight forward. As they passed, he saw the officer's gaze idly follow their car, saw his brow furrow when he noticed Frank's broken window.

They passed him, kept going.

"Kline, roll down your window and put your mirror back in position," said Grida. "We don't want him to have anything to wonder about."

Kline did.

"Good boy," said Grida.

After a few minutes, Kline caught sight of the cruiser in his side mirror, following at a distance. He didn't say anything, just watched.

"Is he following us?" asked Grida.

"No," lied Kline.

"Don't lie to me," said Grida. "This is your only warning. Is he following?"

Kline hesitated, nodded.

"Yes," said Grida. And then, almost to herself, "These men in authority, believing themselves invincible as they edge closer and closer to their own deaths."

They reached a set of railroad tracks, unmown weeds to either side. Frank drove slowly over them. They'd just reached the other side when behind them the cruiser's flashers flipped on, the interior of their car stuttering with red and blue light.

"What do you want me to do?" Frank asked.

"Are you an idiot? What you'd normally do, of course. Pull over."

Frank nodded. He turned his blinker on, slowly slid to the side of the road.

"Now what?" Frank asked.

"Let me handle this," said Grida.

Frank nodded again, slower this time.

"Anything I should know about the car?" asked Grida. "License and registration current?"

"Yes," said Frank. "Everything is in order. It's my car."

Kline cast a glance at the knob of the door lock. There was no way to pull it up without her noticing.

They waited. For a long time the officer didn't come, just stayed there behind them, spotlight on them.

"What's he doing?" asked Grida.

"Calling the plate in, probably," said Frank.

Kline shifted slightly in his seat, awaiting his chance, wondering if it would ever come.

"Any chance he's calling for backup?" asked Grida.

Frank shrugged. "Always a chance," he said. "But not likely."

And indeed, in just a moment more, they heard the sound of a door behind them shutting, then the officer's boots on the gravel of the shoulder as he approached their car.

He stopped beside the driver's side window, bent down.

"Evening," he said.

"Evening," said Frank.

"License and . . ." He trailed off. He reached down and touched the side of the car. When his finger came up, it was dark with the guard's congealed blood.

It was clear from the blankness of his expression that he couldn't quite understand what he was seeing. And then it hit. He stumbled back, fumbling to unsnap his holster. And then the back window burst and so did the man's head. What was left of him sat down heavily on the road, slowly tipped over.

Kline's ears were ringing. "You have to stop doing that!" he shouted.

Frank was yelling. "No need for that!" he was shouting. "No need! I could have worked things out with him. There was no reason for him to die!"

"There doesn't ever have to be a reason. Drive, for Christ's sake," said Grida. "Now."

Frank swore, turned the car on, drove. "They probably have our plates," he said. "They'll know it's us."

"What do I care?" said Grida. "It's not *my* car."

Another ten minutes of driving, the wind whistling now all through one side of the car, bits of pebbled glass occasionally rattling in or down the side of the car, and Grida said, "Slow down."

Frank did. They were far from town now. To their left was a series of fields, each loomed over by massive center pivot irrigation sprinklers. To their right was a chain-link fence, barbed wire strung eccentrically along its top. Beyond the fence was an empty asphalt lot, cracked and with waist-high weeds sticking through, and beyond the lot was a large and dilapidated industrial compound, three overlapping buildings or maybe four, hard to tell exactly from this distance in the darkness.

"Turn in there," said Grida calmly.

A little way along, the fence was punctuated by an opening. Frank pulled up, stopped before a barrier gate right beside a gatehouse.

"Are you going to shoot this guard too?" asked Kline.

"What guard?" asked Grida.

And indeed, there was nobody inside the gatehouse. It was deserted.

They waited. "What do we do?" Frank finally said.

"Be patient," Grida said. "He knows." And when she said this, *he knows*, something different entered her voice, something softer.

They waited, engine rumbling, headlights shining over the cracked asphalt. For a long moment there was nothing, and then, suddenly, out of the darkness, something loomed. Indistinct at first, keeping just outside of the beams of the lights, but gradually becoming larger and larger.

"Frank . . ." said Kline.

"I see him," said Frank.

It was the giant. He held an aluminum bat in his remaining hand, his large fist making it look like a child's toy. He circled the car, slowly, like a dog sniffing out a trail, came to a stop just beside Grida's window.

"Hello, Artem," Grida said.

The giant gave a little whine, then squeezed his way into the gatehouse, opened the barrier gate. Frank drove through. When he started to drive on, Grida stopped him.

"Where are your manners?" she asked.

A moment later, the giant opened the rear passenger door and forced himself in, the car yawing noticeably to one side. He reached up, placing his one big hand on Kline's shoulder.

"Hello, Kline," he said in his hoarse whisper. "A pleasure to see you again."

2.

They pulled up in front of the glass doors of the complex's foremost building. Two well-muscled women were waiting there, like sentries, to either side of the doors. Each was missing an arm, and was armed with an electric cattle prod. When the car pulled up, they came down the steps and toward it.

Grida stepped out of the car. Both sentries bowed to her.

"The prophetess has returned," whispered the giant loudly, clambering out of the car himself.

"The prophetess has returned," repeated the sentries.

"Yes, yes," said Grida. "Of course she has. She always does. This car needs to be disposed of. Artem, handle our friends."

"Kindly exit the vehicle," whispered the giant to Kline and Frank.

Slowly Kline and Frank climbed out. One of the two sentries climbed in. A moment later, the car disappeared behind the building.

As Grida kept the pistol trained on them, the giant searched first Frank and then Kline. He took away Frank's pistol. He searched Kline twice, apparently unable to believe he wasn't carrying a weapon. Finally, he nodded.

“Good,” said Grida. And then to Kline, “Come on, there’s something I want to show you.”

She started up the steps. After a moment, Kline and Frank followed, the giant and the other sentry with the cattle prod just behind.

At the doors, she stopped.

“Not you,” she said to Frank. “Just Kline.”

She opened the door and went inside, not bothering to look back to see if Kline followed. She walked with a rocking motion, as if she wasn’t completely in control of one half of her body—the same half as the weak side of her face. But she had made something elegant, almost hypnotic, of the irregularity. After a moment, the giant prodded Kline toward the doors. Kline opened them and went through, the giant on his heels; he looked back once at Frank standing there on the stairs, forlornly watching him, and then the woman beside Frank touched him with the tip of her cattle prod. Frank fell shuddering to the ground and rolled down the stairs. Kline stopped.

“Keep moving,” whispered the giant.

“What are you going to do to him?”

“I’m not going to do anything to him. I’m coming with you.”

“What’s going to happen to him?”

The giant didn’t answer.

“Was that really necessary?” asked Kline.

“Necessary?” whispered the giant. The way he shaped the word in his mouth made it seem like it was a word he had never considered before. “It happened,” he whispered. “Thus it was necessary.”

They passed through an empty, poorly lit lobby. There were spots where signs for whatever company this complex had once belonged to had been stripped from the walls, leaving only their ghosts behind. The tile of the floor, too, was cracked and broken. Up ahead, at the far end of the lobby, he saw Grida start down a curving hall dotted with occasional doors. Soon she disappeared around a corner. Kline and the giant followed her.

"There's no reason to kill Frank," said Kline.

"Who is to say if there is a reason or no?" whispered the giant. "It is not ours to question."

"His death would be pointless," said Kline.

"Perhaps the pointlessness is the point."

"I don't want him to die."

The giant didn't bother to respond. They followed the curve around. Grida still wasn't visible. The hall was a dirty white, the walls punctuated by doors, the ceiling strung with buzzing fluorescent tubes. He passed one door that was ajar: behind it seemed to be a makeshift dormitory, several women sitting on beds. Another door, this one closed, read CONTROL.

They kept curving gently along the hallway. They must have nearly completed a full circuit, Kline believed, or maybe it just felt that way. If he started running, he wondered, how far would he get before the giant caught him? Probably, he realized, not far at all. There were still doors, they were still passing doors, but these had all been boarded over and painted black. They kept walking, fewer and fewer fluorescents in the ceiling now, the hall dark with shadows. And then, abruptly, they came to the curving hall's end.

There had been a door there, but it was boarded over, just like the others. Instead of being painted completely black, though, this one was white and had a crude red face drawn on it. It had the expressionless broadness of an Olmec sculpture. Kline reached out and touched it, then turned back around to face the giant. Maybe, he suddenly realized, it was he rather than Frank who was in danger of being killed.

But the giant just stood there, as expressionless as the painted head, observing him, making no move.

"Well?" Kline finally said.

"Where did she go?" whispered the giant. "Don't you wonder?"

Kline felt the hairs on his arm begin to rise, both on the arm that was there and on the arm that wasn't. "It's a trick, of course," he said.

"If she doesn't want to be seen, she isn't seen," whispered the giant. "She has taken a curse and made it into a blessing. Don't you believe me?"

"Why does everyone keep trying to convince me that I need to believe?"

"Because you're so ready for belief we feel it dripping off you," said Grida's voice. Kline whirled. She was there, just beside the white and red door, standing in the shadows.

"Where did you go?" he asked.

"Nowhere," she said. "I've been here all along."

"Why didn't I see you?"

"You only see what you want to see."

He brushed past her and into the end of the corridor, looking for an alcove, somewhere she could have hidden, but there was nothing.

"I was standing right there," she said. "When you touched the door, you nearly touched me."

No, he thought. *That's impossible.*

He heard a noise in front of him. The giant had bent down, had grabbed hold of a ring set in the floor. Almost effortlessly, he pulled open a large trapdoor, revealing a set of stairs leading down. Light came streaming up from below.

"All I ask of you, Mr. Kline, is that for a few minutes at least you keep an open mind. Is that too much to ask?"

"It might be," said Kline.

"Would you rather go where your friend Frank is going?"

Kline hesitated. "I don't think so," he finally offered.

"You absolutely wouldn't," whispered Artem.

He went down the stairs. What else could he do? There were lights periodically affixed to the wall running beside the stairs, four in all. Behind him, he heard Grida's distinctive stuttering tread, and behind that, just barely, the remarkably agile whisper of the giant's feet.

The stairs terminated at a metal door.

"Go on," said Grida levelly from behind him. "It's open."

He reached out and depressed the handle. The door swung open. On the other side was a large square room, a door in the middle of the far wall, a door in both side walls as well. A circular mosaic in the floor's center depicted the left half of a female body, neatly bisected, its arm raised to the square.

"Welcome to the Temple Angelic and Triumphant," said Grida.

"Brighter than the sun," whispered the giant.

"Brighter than the sun," said Grida.

"Colder than the moon," said the giant.

"Colder than the moon. Choose a door, Mr. Kline. Any door will do."

"What if I don't want to choose?" said Kline.

"The only thing worse than not choosing would be to have someone choose for you," said Grida.

Kline folded his arm, waited.

"Did we not agree that you would attempt to have an open mind?" And when, after a few minutes, Kline still hadn't moved, "I begin to lose patience, Mr. Kline. Artem?"

Almost before Kline could turn around, the giant was upon him, had slapped him open-handed hard enough to knock him off his feet. Kline got to his knees, fell again when the giant kicked him in the stomach. He rolled gasping onto his back, trying to catch his breath. A moment later, the giant loomed over him, and then he placed his foot on Kline's throat, resting it lightly but firmly there.

"It happened," whispered the giant. "Thus it was necessary." And then, for the first time, Kline saw him smile. His smile was the most terrifying thing about him.

"Choose a door, Mr. Kline," said Grida, from some distance away.

"Far door," he managed to get out between gasps beneath the giant's foot.

"Bad choice! You are not ready for that door," said Grida, irritation in her voice. "Choose another."

"Left."

"Ah," she said. "Yes, very good."

"Very good," repeated the giant, and removed his foot from Kline's throat. He extended a hand and when Kline took it he was pulled abruptly to his feet. The giant held onto him a moment, steadied him until he was sure Kline could stand on his own, and then patted him gently and let go.

"You made the choice," said Grida. "You lead the way."

Grunting, limping a little, Kline made his way toward the door in the left wall.

The door led to a small room, walls painted white, floor white too, the room antiseptically clean. In the room's center was a table with metal legs, its surface painted a shiny white enamel, a shiny white metal chair on either side. One side of the table was more like a desk, with enough room for a person to sit but with a stack of drawers on the left. The other side was more like a table.

Grida moved in her uniquely fluid fashion to the desk side of the table, sat down. She gestured to the other chair. After a moment's hesitation, Kline moved forward and sat.

"Welcome to heaven, Mr. Kline."

"It looks more like an office."

"You'll understand soon enough," said Grida. Behind him, somewhere, Kline knew, lurked the giant. He was there looming, waiting.

She opened the topmost drawer of the stack and took from within it a life-sized rubber hand. She placed it on the desk, palm up. It lay there like a freshly slaughtered beast.

"This what you wanted to show me?" asked Kline, reaching out to touch it. "A rubber hand?"

"It's not rubber," said Grida.

Kline flinched.

"Don't worry," said Grida. "Nothing to be afraid of. It's just a hand. Given willingly. It's perfectly safe. It's been lacquered, preserved, its surface sealed. That's why you mistook it for rubber."

"Whose was it?" asked Kline cautiously, dreading the answer.

"The question is not whose hand was it, but whose hand can it be?"

"Whose hand can it be?"

Grida smiled with half her face, spread what remained of her arms. "Whoever desires it," she said. "Perhaps, great doubter, even you."

"What do I want with it?"

Grida didn't answer. She opened the bottom drawer and removed from it another hand, this one a prosthetic, but with feathers in the place of fingers. She slipped this over the stump of her wrist, tightened the straps with her teeth.

From a final drawer, she took out a long feather. This she held in the hand she still had.

"Pull your chair a little closer," she said.

"Why?" asked Kline.

"The sooner you do, the sooner we can move forward."

Kline sighed, awkwardly tugged his chair closer to the desk.

"Good," Grida said. "There's a channel underneath the desk that you can slide your hand into. Please do so now. Palm up, fingers open, just like the hand on the desk." Kline did so. "Now I want you to extend your missing arm. Line it up best you can with the hand on the desk."

"The severed hand."

"The severed hand," Grida agreed. "Look just at that severed hand. Stare at it. Nothing else."

Kline hesitated, then did as asked. He stared at the hand. He watched as Grida began to stroke the severed hand softly, regularly, with the long feather. The rhythm was almost hypnotic.

He caught a motion out of the corner of his eye. When he started to turn toward it, Grida scolded him. "If you can't keep your gaze on the hand on your own, I'll have to have Artem hold your head still," she said.

Kline turned his gaze back to the hand. "It's not a real hand," he felt compelled to say. Though of course it had been once.

"No," agreed Grida. "Not yet."

She kept stroking the hand. It was strange to watch.

When something touched his hand beneath the table, he flinched a little.

"Just relax," said Grida, her voice soothing now. "Watch the hand on the table. That's the hand that's being touched with the feather. It's your hand. You can see that to be the case."

For a moment he thought, *No, she's stroking my hand beneath the desk.* He knew this must be the case, but then everything lurched, as if the world were slipping out from under him. He could see it. It was there on the desk. It was being stroked with a feather. He could feel it. It was, he felt, his hand. *It's not really my hand*, he tried to tell himself, but he didn't completely believe it. He stared at the hand, and as he stared the air between his shoulder and the severed hand thickened, began to gel, began to shimmer.

Involuntarily, he shivered.

"There!" said Grida, hungrily. "Do you feel it? It's happening."

He did not respond. He hardly heard her. As he watched, a ghostly band of flesh slowly materialized in the air, joining his shoulder to the severed hand on the table. As he watched, as he felt the slow, insistent, rhythmic stroking of the feather on his finger, saw the same stroking on the hand on the table, the shimmering band of flesh grew more and more substantial, more and more real.

"No . . ." said Kline.

"Don't resist it," whispered Grida, her voice hungry now. "Let the miracle take place."

And yet, miracle or no, he couldn't bring himself to give fully in to it. With a groan, he pushed himself away from the desk and stepped back. The shimmering band of flesh stretched, stretched, and then snapped, vanished. He stumbled and nearly fell, felt the giant catch him, cradle him, and then almost effortlessly lift him up in his arms.

And there was Grida's pallid face, peering, perhaps a foot away, expressionless.

"You felt it," she said. "I know you did."

Kline closed his eyes, turned away, buried his face in the giant's chest.

"A good first effort," said Grida. "The first of the mysteries has been unveiled. Artem, I task you with revealing to Kline the second."

• • •

Artem had set him on his feet but still kept his one large hand cupped around the back of Kline's neck, pushing him forward. He propelled Kline back out of the room and into what Kline thought of now as the narthex of the temple, the mosaic of the bisected female body at its center. This time, Artem pushed him toward the right-hand door.

"Are you going to kill me?" asked Kline, stumbling forward.

"Probably," whispered Artem. "Just not yet."

They reached the door and Artem stretched one huge hand past him and turned the handle, then used Kline's body to push the door ajar. Behind was a narrow hall, poorly lit. At the far end was a pebbled metal door with a radial latch instead of a handle. A humming could be heard coming through the door. The sound reminded Kline of something as he walked forward, and then he realized what: the sound of the freezer at the home of the Pauls.

"No," said Kline. "Oh no."

"Yes," whispered Artem, and when Kline tried to break away, the giant tightened his hold around his neck and shook him until his vision began to blur. And then Artem slipped his stump between the door and its latch and opened the door.

A blast of cold air and frost. Artem gave him a shove. Kline stumbled in. He heard the door shutting behind him. He wheeled and ran for it, but was too late: by the time he got there, it was already closed.

There was no handle on this side. He pushed at the door. It didn't open. He pounded, shouted, but nothing changed.

It was very cold, exceptionally so.

He turned and took the room in. On the floor in one corner of the room was Frank. Kline was not sure if he was dead or merely unconscious. His face was bruised, one eye nearly swollen shut.

Kline kneeled beside him, began to shake him. For a long moment he was sure the man was dead, until, finally, he groaned.

"Frank," said Kline. "Get up."

After more shaking, Frank managed to open one eye. And then, groaning again, he pushed Kline away and rolled over onto his belly. He began awkwardly, swaying, to get to his feet. He had to hold onto Kline to stay upright. His teeth were chattering.

"What happened?" asked Kline.

Frank just shook his head. "It's too cold. We have to get out of here."

His gaze kept slipping around the room-sized freezer, looking for something, Kline couldn't see what.

Frank's brow furrowed. "She shocked me," said Frank. "With her prod. Then she kicked me awake and shocked me again. Then I woke up here." He seemed a little steadier now. He stumbled toward the door, began to pound on it with his hand.

"They're not going to open it," said Kline. "They want us here."

"We can't stay," said Frank. "We'll freeze to death."

Probably, Kline thought, they had been put here precisely so that they would freeze to death.

"What do we do?" asked Frank.

"We keep moving," said Kline. "Once we stop moving, we're dead."

They trod a path around the edges of the room, all the while feeling the cold seeping deeper and deeper. At the top of the wall opposite the door was a stainless-steel grate that hummed and spat out cold air. The whole face of the grate was covered in frost.

They kept walking. Frank was having a harder time staying upright, and couldn't keep up. He was shivering all over. Kline was shivering too, though not as bad. Where he had sweated, the fabric of his shirt had frozen, become stiff, brittle.

He wrapped an arm around Frank and pulled him closer, walked with him like that, though whether he did it to keep Frank upright or to help keep himself warm, he would have been hard-pressed to say.

Around and around, the freezer humming the whole time, the room growing colder and colder. Crystals of ice, Kline saw, had begun to form here and there on the walls, and their breath clouded the air. Kline could no longer feel his toes or his fingers. His face had gone numb.

"We're going to die," mumbled Frank.

"Shut up and keep walking," said Kline.

Frank gave a groan of frustration but kept moving. One step then another, one step then another. Kline was shivering uncontrollably now. Was there a way out where the cold air was flowing in, some kind of duct they could climb into or something? No, there didn't seem to be, the ventilation grate was far too small for a human to fit into.

And then he saw it, beside the grate. It had been recessed into the wall, was partly obscured by the cloud of cold air flowing in, but once he saw it, he was certain: the lens of a camera.

"They're watching us," said Kline.

"What?" said Frank, coming out of his deathbound reverie. He looked vaguely around, eyes dull. "Where?" he said. "Who?"

"Up there," said Kline, and gestured to the lens. "They're watching us die."

Was that what it meant? Were Grida and Artem simply in another room, a control room, CONTROL, elsewhere in the compound, staring at a screen, observing them, waiting for them to collapse? What was it the giant had said when Kline had asked if he was going to kill him? *Probably. Only not yet.*

Well then, how about now?

Frank staggered and fell to one knee. "So cold," he whispered.

"Keep walking," said Kline. "Don't stop," he said, despite wanting to stop himself.

His mind began, slowly, to float away. It was as if he were watching his body from slightly above, from slightly outside his skin, instead of inside. There his body was below him, arms clasped around Frank, plodding along. How long would they be able to stay upright? Probably not long, but he'd have to try, he'd have to—

Wait.

He found himself suddenly rooted in his body again, no longer above. His *arms* clasped around Frank? But he had only one full arm. And yet when he looked down he saw two. One seemed like an ordinary arm. The other was of a different substance than flesh, or was of flesh shot through with light, a strange luminous thing.

I'm hallucinating, he told himself. Yet it didn't feel like he believed a hallucination should feel. The arm felt *real.*

Beside him, Frank stepped wrong and sagged. For a moment, Kline tried to hold him up, and then, realizing he might go down with him, he let Frank fall.

Frank collapsed in a heap and lay there groaning, moving ever so slightly. Kline held out his actual arm and his new, perhaps imagined, arm and stared at them. The new arm began to shimmer. He turned it this way and that, examining the fingers at the end of it. It was real but not real—both real and not at the same time. Unless it was simply, as he had first believed, a hallucination.

He was still standing motionless, still staring at his hands, the one that was probably there and the one that probably wasn't, when the door swung open. The giant was standing in the doorframe. He had to stoop and sidle to make his way through.

"Have you come to kill me?" asked Kline. His tongue felt thick and dead in his mouth.

"You?" whispered Artem. "No."

"You've felt it," said Grida's voice from the doorway. "I could tell even through the monitor."

"Felt what?"

"The return of the missing. The arrival of the holy spirit."

Was that what it was? Face numb, brain numb, Kline stared again at his hands. They looked the same to him now. He could not tell which hand was still there, if either of them were.

"What's happening to me?" he asked.

"You are being purified by the cold," said Grida. "*In extremis veritas*. I was right about you, Kline. So were all those others who saw glory in you, even if they did not know how properly to nourish that glory. You have been through the refiner's fire and have come out a new being. Only in this case the refiner's fire is ice."

"Some say the world will end in fire," murmured Artem. "Some say in ice."

"Yes," said Grida, and laid a hand gently on the giant's arm. Was it, Kline wondered, the hand she still had? Or was he seeing a hand that was no longer there?

The giant reached out a hand to him. "Come," he whispered.

Kline, befuddled, began to reach for him, but then hesitated. "What about Frank?"

"What about him?" asked Grida. "He has had the same opportunities as you have had."

"He who lives," claimed Artem, "is less than salt, less than stone."

"What does that even mean?"

"Shhhh," said Grida, but Kline was not sure if she was trying to soothe him or stop the giant from speaking.

"You live," whispered the giant. "And you are less for it. The other does not."

"He's still alive. I'm not leaving without him," said Kline.

For a moment, there, just inside the doorway, Artem and Grida just stared at him, motionless, no expressions on their faces at all. It was as if they were bodies waiting for a spirit to occupy them. And then they both turned to face one another. After a moment, Grida gave a brief nod.

Very carefully and slowly, the giant cracked his neck and stretched his arms, and then he came for Kline.

Kline stepped back, stumbled over Frank's body, almost went down. He moved backward, realizing only too late that the giant was forcing him into a corner. He feinted left and cut right, tried to rush past, but the giant's hand was already grasping the fabric of his shirt. He tried to shake loose, strip out of the shirt. But Artem was lifting him off the ground, tucking him under one arm as if he were a rag doll. Kline, remaining fingers and toes numb, struggled weakly. Artem carried him out of the room. As Artem held him immobilized, Grida shut the door.

"What's going to happen to Frank?" asked Kline.

"What do you think?" whispered Artem.

"You'll see him again," said Grida. "I promise."

"Promise?"

Grida shrugged. "Sure, I promise." And then she added, "Eventually."

Artem carried Kline to the edge of the mosaic in the middle of the room, then spilled him into its center.

Kline groaned, struggled to rise to his feet, but found the giant had placed a foot on his chest.

"Stay," he said. "Rest. Sleep."

And, somehow, exhausted, chilled to the core, extremities tingling and prickling as they became alive again, he did.

He woke up sore, one arm aching. He was, he saw, from the colored tiles beside his eye, still in the mosaic. He turned his head and saw, there, squatting effortlessly just outside of the circle, Artem.

"How does it feel to be alive?" asked the giant in his hoarse whisper.

"Where's Frank?" asked Kline.

The giant frowned. "That's not an answer to my question."

"I wasn't—" started Kline.

"Be quiet," said Artem.

For a long moment Kline stared at him, hunkered there just outside the ring of the mosaic.

"What are you getting out of this?" he finally asked.

"This?" asked the giant, confused.

"You know," said Kline. "All this. Serving Grida. Doing her will."

"Salvation," the giant whispered without hesitation.

The sincerity of the response startled Kline.

"Why serve Grida?" asked Kline. "Why not just take charge yourself?"

"I'm not a prophetess," the giant whispered. "I do not hear God. The Prophetess Grida does."

"There's no such thing as a prophetess," said Kline. "Grida is the same as you and me."

The giant smiled, that same terrible smile. "Get thee behind me, Satan."

Kline tried again. "There's nothing beyond this world."

The giant shook his head. "I know you know better," he said. "I glimpsed understanding in you."

Kline opened his mouth to speak, then closed it again. His missing hand was still tingling. He was worried that if he looked down he would still see something there.

"The devil came to the son of God in his suffering," whispered Artem. "He lifted him up and showed him all the world. 'Bow down to me,' he said, 'and all that you see shall be yours.' Are you the devil, Brother Kline? Have you come to tempt me?"

"Are you the son of God?" asked Kline.

And then, before Artem could answer, impossibly, appearing as if out of thin air, there was Grida, just beside the giant. Kline couldn't help but flinch when she appeared.

Grida smiled with half of her mouth. "Hello, Mr. Kline," she said.

"Stop doing that!" said Kline.

"Doing what?" she asked. Slowly her mouth curled into that half smile again. "You think it a trick," she said. "What if I were to tell you that what I am doing is crossing out of this mortal world and into the world beyond, the one where your missing arm lives? I stay there, peering into this world and then, at just the right moment, I cross back."

"I'd say you were lying," said Kline.

"Always the great unbeliever," she said. "Like Thomas in the Bible. Will you doubt the evidence of your own eyes? You would do well to remember, Doubter, that even Doubting Thomas was converted in the end."

Kline said nothing.

"Tell me, when you were very cold, when your brain was shutting down, when you were approaching that dark bridegroom, death, what did you see?"

"Nothing," said Kline quickly.

She shook one finger at him, slowly. "Such a bad liar, Kline. Something changed for you. We watched it change, we saw you staring at the hand that was no longer there and saw you see it there nonetheless. You parted the veil! You opened the curtain and saw on the other side that portion of you that had passed beyond."

"No," said Kline.

"Yes," said Grida. "Which is, to be frank, the only reason why you are still alive." She half-smiled. "To be *frank*," she said. "Perhaps an unfortunate choice of words. Shall we go see how things have turned out? Will you come worship with us?"

And when Kline didn't respond: "Artem?" she said.

With one fluid movement Artem reached into the circle and plucked Kline up.

3.

Artem carried him, crushed against his side. Kline could hardly breathe. When he struggled, Artem squeezed him tighter and then he really couldn't breathe. For a moment he struggled desperately but this only made Artem squeeze tighter and then tighter still. Kline eventually fell slack. After a moment Artem allowed him to breathe again.

"Oye! Oye!" Artem whispered. "Come one, come all."

They moved slowly across the room.

"You have progressed through two doors," whispered Artem. "The right, and then the left. Where do you suppose you shall go now?"

Kline tried to speak, but he was still being pressed too tight against the giant's chest to say anything coherent. He grunted into the giant's shirt.

"That's right," whispered Artem. "The central door. The temple's inner sanctum. The door you were not allowed to pass through before. But you shall go through it now."

"And if I don't want to?" Kline managed to get out.

"What?" said Artem, as if genuinely surprised. "Oh, no. Too late for that. You're going through."

They reached the central door. Artem set him gently on the ground and then knocked, striking his meaty hand three times against the metal of the door. The door opened slightly, revealing a woman's face.

"What is wanted?" she asked.

It was not, so far as Kline could tell from this vantage, a woman he had met before. Her hair was hidden under a bandeau, as if she were a nun. Perhaps she was.

"I bring Kline," whispered the giant, "he is ready to worship." And hearing that, the woman stepped aside and admitted them.

They passed into a hallway. It was dark there, one dim bulb illuminating the whole of the corridor. At the far end was a door. Kline found himself pushed by Artem toward it.

The hallway was cold, but not uncomfortably so. The door at the far end was almost obscured by darkness, hardly visible. Somehow this reassured him.

"Come one, come all!" said a voice from just outside the door, a voice that was not completely familiar, from a shadowy, berobed figure. "Gather round."

"Gather round what?" asked Kline.

His interlocutor fumbled for a moment, not quite able to decide how best to respond.

And then Grida appeared, just beside him. One moment she wasn't there and then suddenly she was. She bowed deeply, and Kline saw there were now, in the shadows beside him, a dozen women in long, thick dark robes, plus himself and the giant. Where had they all come from?

"Shall we go in, sisters?" asked Grida.

"We shall go in," all repeated in unison, including Artem. Only Kline remained silent.

He was being prodded to follow the others to the door at the far end. When they reached the door, they halted en masse. The women spread to either side, lining the walls of the hall, and allowed Grida to come to the fore.

She approached the door, placed one hand on the latch. It was the same sort of radial latch as that of the freezer he had just been in, though the door itself was bigger. "Shall we open the door and proceed to the inner sanctum?" she asked.

"We shall open the door!" said the worshippers in unison.

"No," said Kline. "Leave it closed."

"So let it be written, so let it be done," said Grida, and threw open the door.

A blast of frigid air, a cloud of deadly frost. For the rest of his life Kline remembered periodically what it had been like, that blast of cold and cloud of frost and then, slowly, as they all filed in, the air clearing to reveal what the room contained.

The giant had his hand closed tight around Kline's upper arm, his grip impossibly big. He propelled Kline forward. In front of them, the women and Grida cut to the left and right to form a circle around the center of the room.

There was something there, but Kline wasn't sure what it was. He was, at first, unable to see it clearly over the circle of women. They were humming: a strange, low sound. What he could see, however, was that around the circumference of the room was a series of hooks attached to the ends of cables anchored to the ceiling. From most of these hooks hung a body. Or, rather, half a body.

"We kept the half we needed," said Grida. She was staring at him, watching him, waiting to see how he would respond. "We gave your friend Gous the other halves to see if he could learn to use them, perhaps be led to the true path. Unfortunately for him, he could not."

She gestured up with a flourish of her chin. Kline lifted his gaze and saw Gous's other half. It swung gently on its hook, its ice-encrusted innards revealed.

It seemed to him colder in this room than the other, almost unbearably so. But neither Grida nor the worshippers seemed to feel the cold.

"Come," said Grida.

She took his hand and Kline, numb, let himself be led forward. The circle before them parted and they entered within its circumference. Inside was a long metal table of industrial design. Frank was lying atop it, hand at his side.

"See?" said Grida. "I told you you would see him again."

Kline didn't respond.

"We are here for the hoisting," said Grida to the crowd around them. "This is a joyous day."

"A joyous day!" the crowd repeated.

"The hoisting?" said Kline. And then, his own hand tugged by Grida's hand, he moved, as if in a trance, closer, and finally saw clearly what was on the table.

The giant caught up to him before he'd made it even halfway across the temple narthex.

"Where are you going?" he whispered. "The service hasn't even begun."

"No," said Kline. "Let me go. Please."

"Ahh," whispered the giant. "We both know that won't happen. Be a good boy and come with me."

Kline resisted, but it did him no good. He dug his heels in, tried to resist. At first, Artem just dragged him, but eventually he tired of this and slapped Kline's head until his ears rang.

Even then, Kline resisted. "No," he said, "I don't want to see."

"You have to see," whispered the giant. "You are here to witness." And then, after a moment, "Besides, you have already seen."

Soon they were back at the table. It was, Kline now realized, a table saw, arranged as if it were an altar in the center of the room. The circle of women parted as the giant forced Kline to approach, bringing him to the very edge of the table.

Frank's body had been frozen solid and then cut bilaterally, split exactly down the middle. The saw blade rested there, right in the middle of his forehead. A hole had been bored through the fabric covering each scapula, no doubt for the insertion of a hook.

He immediately closed his eyes, but it was too late. The image was already burned into his brain. Swaying, he turned away. It was pointless, awful.

"Ah," said Grida. "Welcome back, Kline. We no longer have somewhere to send the half we don't need. Shall we give it to you?"

Kline couldn't bring himself to give any response at all.

Grida laughed softly after a moment. "As you wish," she said. And then, "Let the hoisting begin."

Later, he was hard-pressed to explain to himself what exactly he had experienced. It was freezing, very cold, but none of the women nor Grida nor the giant were shivering. He was the only one who was shivering. Perhaps the women's robes were thicker and warmer than they looked, but they were in any case barefoot, and Grida was not wearing a robe, nor was Artem. Chanting, they lifted the left half of Frank off the table saw and, with a certain amount of struggle, slowly raised him up and lined up the hole in his back with one of the empty hooks, the one just adjacent to Gous, and affixed him to it. He swung there, grotesque, body turning to reveal by turns his complete half and his missing one.

"Come," said Grida. "Stand with us."

Not knowing what else to do, Kline did.

Grida began to hum, raising her arm, letting it fall, raising it, letting it fall. The women around them did the same. Kline just stayed motionless and dumb, getting colder and colder.

And then Grida uttered a certain phrase, one that went out of his mind almost as soon as it entered it, but still somehow stayed resonating in the emptiness it left. She snapped her fingers twice, the sound as brittle as sticks snapping, and Kline's world changed.

I've been hypnotized, thought Kline, and then ceased to think this as he saw what was there around him, took it in gasping. Along the walls, the bodies on hooks began to transform. He could see, glowing, their missing halves. The missing half of Frank's face was smiling, wreathed in ecstasy. It was both wonderful and terrible to behold.

He turned and saw the worshippers circled around the table saw that was, of course, he now realized, an altar after all. They were facing outward, their missing limbs glowing as well, at once present and absent. And there was Grida, her arm made whole again, an arm of pure light now, shimmering, holy. When she moved now there was no hitch in her step. And inside the ring, on the altar, was the other half of Frank's body, and this too had regained its missing half. Frank was hanging whole from a hook above him and yet was somehow whole on the altar too.

He couldn't breathe. Grida's twisted face, once paralyzed, had relaxed. When she smiled her whole face smiled. *I have to leave*, he thought, but the giant was there, right behind him, calmly observing him.

"Sisters!" cried Grida. "Sisters! God is here among us! Give in to Her! Let Her be your eyes!"

She reached out with her missing arm, reached forward and stroked Kline's face with glowing fingers, and he felt it.

No, he thought. *This isn't real.*

And then she turned and closed the fingers of her missing hand around the edge of the table saw. She strained with effort, and Kline saw her glowing, missing arm lift one side of the altar off the ground.

He fainted.

When he awoke he was warm again. He was sprawled once more on the floor mosaic. It was like he had never left it. Perhaps, he couldn't help but hope, he hadn't.

Grida was there, her face just beside him, mere inches away. She was staring at him with glittering, unblinking eyes.

"You saw it," she said.

He hesitated, then nodded. She smiled.

"You know now what we can do," she said. "We have torn the curtain between this world and the next. Do you acknowledge this?"

He hesitated. "It certainly seems that way," he said carefully.

"You must join us," she said. "Will you join us?"

He shook his head.

"No?" she said, confused. "Why not? But you saw, you know."

"I don't want to," Kline said. "*Non serviam.*"

She pursed the lips on one side of her face in disapproval. "You know who first said those words?"

"I know," said Kline. "Satan."

"You would choose the devil over something you have seen with your own eyes?"

"The devil is safer," said Kline. Slowly he sat up. Grida, however, remained close, didn't withdraw at all. She shook her head.

"You are a puzzle, Kline," she said. "We're committed to the same things. We both want to destroy the Brotherhood. You have seen us pierce the veil. You have seen a missing, insubstantial arm lift a physical object. You know we have power. Despite all this, you won't join us?"

"I won't," said Kline.

"Do you reject the evidence of your own senses?"

"I hope it's a trick," he said. "I am terrified it might not be."

She shook her head. "Lukewarm," she said. "You follow the whirling banner. I know thy works, that thou art neither cold nor hot: I would thou wert cold or hot." She grinned with half of her face. "I will spew thee out of my mouth." She looked over Kline's head. "Artem," she said.

"Yes, prophetess?" whispered Artem from behind him.

"We cannot make him warm," said Grida. "And so we must make him very cold indeed. Take him away. Spew him out of God's mouth."

The giant dragged him back to the sanctum with the halved bodies and the table saw altar and thrust him in, sent him once again sprawling.

Aching, Kline regained his feet. The giant stood there, filling the doorway.

"She wants you to think about what you believe."

"I don't believe in anything," Kline lied.

Artem ignored this. "You have one last chance," he said. "If even that." And then he swung shut the freezer door.

4.

I'm going to die, thought Kline. There was the cold air pouring in through the vent, the icy, whitened air. He wrapped his arm around his body, shivering. He would, he feared, soon see his other arm wrapped around his body as well, the one that wasn't there.

Why? Is it really always there, the ghost of it, even with the fleshy arm gone? Was that so hard to believe? Perhaps it was some sort of post-hypnotic suggestion. Something explicable anyway—something with a rational explanation to it, a way he was being manipulated by Grida. How could it be anything but that?

But what if it is real? a growing part of him couldn't help but wonder.

He was walking, shivering, trying to keep moving, to keep warm. His face had gone numb. The humming of the freezer felt now like it was coming from beneath his skin. He imagined his body cut in two, one half hanging from a hook in the air above him, the other half discarded. He looked up, saw Frank, saw Gous, saw other half-bodies of people he didn't know, surrounding him, hemming him in. Had a shimmering in the air begun next to each of them? Were they becoming whole again?

He shook his head. He couldn't think, it was too cold to think. When he blinked, he could feel his lids scrape over his eyes.

I'm going to die, he thought again. He kept walking, shivering. He could see his missing arm now, pale and transparent. It felt cold too, even though it wasn't there. His brain wasn't working well. The giant had said he'd have one last chance. *Maybe*, he'd added. When would that chance come, if ever? Did he want it? Would he really be given it?

When his missing arm became visible, he went to the table saw and switched it on. It made a whirring, humming noise that joined the humming of the freezer unit beneath his skin. He extended his absent arm and pushed it through the blade.

The sound the saw was making didn't change, but the glowing arm came loose and flopped onto the table, an independent creature. And yet it was still attached to him as well, still glowing.

He cut it off a half dozen times until he had a pile of glowing insubstantial limbs, a merry heap. It gave him an incomprehensible satisfaction to see them there, to know he was responsible for them.

The fingers of his real hand, if real was the right word, were very numb. He could barely move them. It was almost as if he didn't have a hand at all.

He flexed the fingers of his glowing absent hand, and all the fingers of all the hands on all the severed arms heaped on the table moved too. His mind too was feeling like it was no longer inside his body, was feeling like it was looming above him, staring down. The only thing within him was the humming. It took a tremendous effort to force his mind back down, to keep it from drifting entirely away.

He shook his head. His remaining hand, the fleshy one, was resting on the table, very close to the spinning, vibrating blade. He pulled the hand back—or tried to anyway: in the cold it had become stuck to the metal of the table. He had to wrench and tear it free.

The pain of this was enough to sharpen him. His mind became lodged within his flesh again, his missing arm in all its iterations was no longer present, the pile of arms on the table saw vanished. He could think again. What he thought was: *Am I the sort of person who will wait to see if I am offered one last chance? Who will wait until I collapse for Grida to decide whether to send Artem in to save me?*

No, he thought, *I have always been the sort of person to make my own chances.*

He examined the table saw. A metal cabinet was part of its subhousing, but it was locked, and without tools he couldn't pop the drawer. Removing the blade from the saw would require an Allen wrench. There was probably one inside the cabinet, but if there was he couldn't get to it.

What else was there? The bodies were hanging on hooks. Could he use a hook? He examined one that didn't have a body on it—perhaps the one saved for him. It was at the end of a cable, the cable itself anchored into the ceiling. He could reach the hook, just barely, and could see that the end of the cable had been attached to it with sturdy metal clips. It was not something he could separate. He could not get the hook off, not without tools. Maybe if he were less exhausted and had two arms he could climb the cable and somehow screw the anchor out of the ceiling, but he doubted it.

That was it, then. There was nothing left. He would have to remain here either until he collapsed and Grida sent Artem to save him or, if she decided not to save him, until he was as cold and frozen as the halved bodies that surrounded him.

As soon as he thought this, he realized there was still a place left to look for help.

He moved as quickly as he could from half-body to half-body, standing with his back to the camera in the hope that they wouldn't be able to clearly see what he was doing. About half the bodies were naked, stripped of clothing, but the others had been cut in half while wearing their clothing, perhaps because once the fabric had frozen to their flesh it was hard to remove without damaging the body beneath. Clothed and naked bodies alternated in sequence—there was no doubt a religious significance to this, but what exactly it was, Kline had no idea.

He rapidly searched the clothed half-bodies, rifling through the pockets that remained. They were stiff, frozen, hard to force his fingers into. The first few were empty, nothing at all, and then he found, in the back jeans pocket of one half-corpse, a wallet. Not what he needed, but he slipped it into his own back pocket anyway. The next had a set of keys—he took these with his numb fingers and slipped them into his own pocket: maybe he could use them as a weapon, or as a tool to remove the saw blade. The next one was Gous, and he was nude. It made Kline dizzy to look at the remains of this person he had known. And then there was Frank, another person he had known. Kline steeled himself to reach into the ex-policeman's pocket and came up with another set of keys. That was it, then. Not much to work with. But wait, there was something else in the pocket as well, something hard and cylindrical, maybe a pocketknife—maybe even a Swiss Army knife with multiple tools and blades. But when, excited, he finally managed to work it out with his numb fingers, he saw it was not a knife at all: it was Frank's disposable lighter.

For a moment he just stared at it, his cold-slowed mind forced to recalibrate itself to move away from what he expected to see and toward what was actually there. *Some say the world will end in fire*, the giant had whispered, *some in ice.* They had chosen ice.

Which left fire to him.

He would have to move quickly. He would only have a few minutes. He would start with the ones that were not visible to the camera, the ones along the wall the camera was affixed to. Perhaps they would realize something was happening, but it might take a moment for them to realize they were seeing smoke, particularly if the monitor the camera was connected to was black and white or had a lower resolution.

There were three bodies along that wall, two of them clothed. He'd have to hope that the clothed ones would catch flame and that they'd make the unclothed one between them catch as well. The bodies were open and there was enough fat exposed that it might be possible. At very least, once they realized what he was doing, they would come in. From there, he would have to improvise.

It was hard to flick the lighter with his numbed thumb. Impossible, almost. He kept moving the wheel, watching the thumb as if it were somebody else's thumb, willing that person, whoever they were, to make the thumb move. A snntch sound, and a few sparks came. He told the thumb it needed to spin the sparkwheel and then hold the fork down so that fuel would feed the flame. The thumb tried again, snntch, sparks. Again, snntch, sparks. Again, snntch, sparks—but a flame too, finally.

The arm moved the flame down to the cuff of the half-body's pantleg. The hand held it there, waiting for the flame to catch. There was one awful moment when it didn't and Kline began to doubt. What if it was his missing hand holding the lighter, the flame only the ghost of a flame? His hand wavered and the flame dipped but he managed to keep the fork partly depressed so the flame didn't go out. And then, as if by magic, a bluish flame began to flicker up the denim of the jeans.

He moved to the next clothed body, not daring to release the fork even though he could see that the top of his thumb had started to blacken. By the time he got the khakis on that body alight, the smoke rising from them darker, stinking, the first body was fully aflame.

And then the lighter flickered and ran out of fuel and sputtered out.

He let it fall to the ground.

What had they called it, the dried murderer's hand that in the Middle Ages thieves stole from a grave and then lit on fire as a way of slowing or stopping time so they could steal with impunity? That they believed would paralyze all but the one who had lit it as long as it was burning? Hand of Glory. Well, then, these were Bodies of Glory. Perhaps as long as they burned Grida and the giant wouldn't come. He warmed his hand in front of the one closest to him. His fingers were beginning to feel like they belonged to him again. The smell of burning flesh was making his mouth water.

What now? He stripped off his shirt, held it to a burning body until it caught flame too, and then hurried from one remaining clothed body to the next, to the next. He managed to get two more lit before he heard shouting from outside the door. He draped his burning shirt over the third body and quickly retreated behind the table saw.

The door opened. Artem. He coughed, waved the smoke away from his face. Only then did Kline realize that he too was having a hard time breathing, that his lungs were full of smoke, his eyes watering.

"No," whispered the giant, "no!"

He lumbered into the room, moved first toward one burning corpse, then another, then stopped, turned his gaze on Kline.

"It was not foretold," whispered the giant. And then he said, "You!"

He came for Kline, but Kline kept the table saw between the two of them. When the giant circled, Kline circled too. Artem was coughing more than him. He was taller, further off the ground, his head higher in the smoke. Kline crouched, came further out of the smoke.

"You've ruined everything," whispered Artem, and coughed.

"I tend to do that," said Kline.

They circled one another, the room filling with smoke.

"You can't reach me," said Kline, "not with the table saw between us. But you can save a few bodies before they burn."

Artem glanced around the room. Four bodies were burning, and the body between each pair was cooking, smoldering. Six more hadn't caught yet.

"Six is enough," managed the giant.

And then, muscles straining, Artem began to push against the table saw.

With a screech it began to grate across the floor, slowly pushing Kline back toward the wall. For a moment Kline hesitated, catching his balance, and then he braced himself and pushed back.

Another screech. The table saw still slid toward him, but just inches this time. Kline, panting, reset his stance and braced himself again.

"You can't win," whispered the giant.

"No," said Kline. "But I can slow you enough for all the bodies to catch fire."

The giant hesitated. Kline could almost see the gears working in his head.

"You can catch me later," said Kline. "You can always catch me."

"Of course I can," whispered the giant. He bent his head down and pushed again. The table saw slid toward Kline another few inches, despite Kline pushing back as hard as he could.

"You're just going to let them burn?" asked Kline. "What kind of believer are you?"

Artem didn't respond, just leaned in and pushed. Kline lost another six inches.

From the doorway came a piercing shriek. Grida was there, hand covering her mouth. Artem hesitated, whirled toward her.

"Save them!" Grida commanded. "Save them!"

And suddenly the giant was gone. Kline watched him rush from body to body, using his one big hand to tear a body off its hook and then, if it was aflame, smother it against his chest. In little more than a moment there were three bodies on the floor and the giant's shirt was smoking, threatening to catch fire.

Kline bolted for the door.

Artem lunged for him, missed. At the doorway Grida began to swing the door closed, but when she realized that Kline would reach it before it shut, she slipped behind the door and out of sight.

Kline dragged the door open and reached for her, but she wasn't there. The hall was empty. He rushed down it and found her somehow already halfway across the mosaic room, moving as fast as she could with her elegant rocking motion.

"Grida!" shouted Kline.

She didn't turn, but for a moment the rocking motion became chaotic. Down the stairs and through the open door clattered two worshippers.

"Stop him!" Grida shrieked, and both women rushed past Grida and toward him.

He dodged the first, swept the other's legs out from under her. She fell, wailing. The first was clawing at him now, nails cutting into the flesh of his bare frostbit back. He swung around and elbowed her in the jaw, hard enough to make his arm fall numb. Jaw hanging loose, eyes rolling up into her head, she collapsed. He kicked the other one again for good measure and she curled in on herself. He ran for the stairs.

Grida had disappeared. He clattered up the darkened stairs. The trapdoor at the top was closed. Was Grida strong enough to open and close it on her own? Could she have already gone through? He didn't think so, considering her partial paralysis. But perhaps she'd had help? Other worshippers following the first two? Or maybe she'd gone another way while he'd been fighting the women? If that was the case, next time he saw her she'd have her gun, and he already knew she was an exceptionally good shot.

He reached toward the trapdoor to open it, but then stopped. Something was different. What was it?

Take your time, he told himself. *Think it through.*

But he didn't have time. Artem would be after him at any moment. He should stop thinking about Grida and flee.

He reached for the trapdoor again, began to open it, and then it came to him: the stairway was too dark. When he'd first descended the staircase there'd been four lights along the side, but the second and fourth lights were now extinguished. More than extinguished: if he squinted against the darkness around them he could see that from each socket hung the shards of a broken bulb.

He let go of the trapdoor, turned around. He held his breath, tried to sense something in the air, tried to hear the sound of someone breathing.

There was a commotion in the mosaic room and Artem appeared at the bottom of the stairs. He was covered in ash, his hair mostly burned off.

"Kline," he whispered. "Come down here so I can kill you."

Kline hesitated, waited. Neither he nor Artem moved.

Very slowly he descended a step, eyes on Artem the whole time.

"Perhaps we can talk this through," said Kline.

"Perhaps," said Artem hoarsely. "Stranger things have happened. Come down and we'll see."

Kline descended another step, then another. He was passing through the first pool of shadow now. Was it that one? No, it wouldn't be that one. Or if it was, he couldn't sense her at all.

"Where are the others?" Kline asked.

"The worshippers? I sent one of the two you hurt to make sure the bodies you tried to burn were extinguished. The second is still unconscious. You broke her jaw. The others are no doubt in the dormitories above."

"What about Grida?" asked Kline.

"What about her?" said Artem.

Three more steps down, not too fast, not too slow. He was coming through the area still lit by a working light bulb. Soon he would pass out of it and into the next band of shadow.

"Where is she?" asked Kline.

Artem didn't answer.

Kline came down another step, and then another. He was in shadow now. At the bottom of the stairs he saw, just barely, almost imperceptibly, Artem grow tense, which is how he knew to reach into the deepest shadow beside him and pull Grida out.

5.

The giant started toward him, mounting a step in the time it took Kline to wrap his arm around Grida's neck, pressing firmly enough against her throat that it was hard for her to breathe, pressing up on her chin from below so she couldn't speak.

"One more step and I snap her neck," said Kline.

Artem stopped, stayed staring at Kline, his body tense.

"It is not prophesied," said Artem.

"Then that probably means you don't take another step."

They waited, neither moving.

"Now take a step down to the floor," said Kline. "And then a few steps away from the bottom of the stairs."

Slowly, reluctantly, Artem did. "Good," said Kline. "Very good. We're being reasonable. Or at least you are. Nobody has to get hurt."

"What do you want?" whispered Artem.

"What does anyone want except to stay alive?"

"Fine," whispered Artem. "Stay alive, then. You can go free. Now release the prophetess."

"I think I'll have to keep her a little longer," said Kline. "Just in case."

Artem said nothing, just flexed his huge hand.

"What I intend to do," said Kline, "is very slowly back my way up the stairs. I'll open the trapdoor, and then Grida and I will leave. Once I feel safe, I promise to set her free."

"When will you feel safe?" asked Artem.

When? thought Kline. Probably the answer was never. But maybe he'd feel safe enough in a day or two, as long as he was at a sufficient distance away to make good on his promise.

He said none of this to Artem. To Artem, all he said was, "I'll know when the right moment is. I won't hurt her."

After a moment's hesitation, Artem reluctantly nodded.

He took a step up and backward, dragging her with him. She struggled, but she couldn't break free.

"She brought you here because she believed you to be special," whispered the giant. "Holy, even."

"That's the mistake they've all made," said Kline.

"She truly believed it," said Artem. "She didn't at first, was skeptical, but time and study convinced her."

"I'm sure that wasn't her first mistake."

"You *are* special," whispered Artem. "She was right about that. But you're not holy. You're the devil. You hate righteousness. You lay waste to everything good you touch."

Kline didn't bother to respond to this, although he didn't altogether disagree. He went up another step, dragging Grida with him.

"No," whispered Artem.

"No?"

"I need to hear the prophetess tell me to let you go."

"Why?"

"Because she's the prophetess. She's the one I serve. She has to tell me to let you go."

Kline stopped, considered. He leaned close to Grida, whispered in her ear: "Do you promise to behave if I loosen my grip a little?" A moment's hesitation, and then he felt her nod against his arm. "Do you promise to tell Artem what he needs to hear and no more? To keep yourself alive?" Another nod, quicker in coming this time.

He loosened his grip just a little. Grida gasped, sucked in air. The giant stepped up a step, then stopped as Kline tightened his grip on Grida's neck again.

"Tell him," said Kline, loud enough for Artem to hear, and then he braced himself and slowly loosened his grip on her neck again.

Very calmly, she took a deep breath. And then she screamed at the top of her lungs, "Kill him!"

He cut off her breath. For a brief moment Artem, startled, remained transfixed, and then he began lumbering up the stairs. There was nowhere for Kline to go.

"Not another step!" he yelled, but Artem kept coming.

And so, not knowing what else to do, Kline twisted his arm as hard as he could and broke Grida's neck.

Artem caught the body as it fell from Kline's arm and began to slide down the stairs. He did so almost tenderly. Kline, arm cocked back, braced himself for his assault, but Artem ignored him. He simply shifted Grida's body until it was lying in the crook of his remaining arm and against his chest. She looked almost as if she were sleeping, as long as you didn't look at her open eyelids and the way each eye stared in a different direction.

Artem looked up the stairs at Kline briefly, no expression on his face whatsoever, and then turned and carried Grida's corpse back into the temple. *He will lay her down in the mosaic*, Kline thought, but Artem walked through it and moved past. *Where, then?* Kline wondered, though he was afraid he knew. He couldn't stop himself from descending a few steps so that he could see where the giant was going.

The giant moved with a slow and stately tread through the door at the far end of the room and into the hall beyond. *Curiosity killed the Kline*, Kline thought, and then went down a few more steps, stepped into the narthex. The worshipper with the broken jaw was slumped on the edge of the mosaic, just beginning to groan.

He skirted around her and moved quietly after Artem. He could see him, just barely, there at the far end of the hall. He followed. The giant balanced Grida's body in one arm and slid his stump into the half-open door, pushed it wider, shouldered his way in.

Kline, despite knowing it was a mistake, followed.

The worshipper inside shrieked as she saw what Artem was carrying. A moment later she rushed out and past him, hardly noticing him, distraught. Kline stepped gingerly down the hall until he reached the doorway and then leaned forward and looked in.

The bodies that had been hung on hooks were now arranged in a line along one wall, touching one another, with their missing half uppermost. The room still smelled of smoke and burnt flesh, and most of the bodies that had been clothed were charred and blackened, the clothing burned off or burned in such a way as to become fused with the flesh. As the bodies had warmed, some of their innards had begun to spill out, and Kline could see where the worshipper had tried to shove them back in place as the half-bodies began to refreeze. What had been planed, smooth surfaces were now irregular and lumpy.

Artem carried Grida to the table saw and laid her carefully down. He went to the far side of the table and pushed the table saw altar back to where it had been before, in the center of the room. He straightened the body, set the head in place, pressed the arms down against the sides. He lined her up with the saw blade and then fell still. He was, Kline realized, waiting for her to freeze.

For a long moment Artem just stared at the body, and then, without forewarning, he looked straight at Kline.

"Shut the door," he whispered. "Leave this place. Now."

And Kline did.

Long before the body was fully frozen, long before Artem turned on the table saw and made Grida into a holy relic, Kline had climbed through the trapdoor and into the curving hall above. He hurt and injured other worshippers as he felt was necessary whenever he crossed their paths, but mostly when they saw him coming, they fled. Maddened and bloody and frostbit, he must have been a sight to behold.

It was night outside, he realized as he approached the glass outer doors. He burst through them and skittered down the steps and managed to wrest the cattle prod from the nearest sentry and use it on her before the other sentry could use hers on him. Soon, he used it on the second sentry as well, and then he waited until the first sentry was sufficiently recovered that she could be tortured into telling him where Frank's car was.

He didn't have the keys. He hot-wired the car and drove. He was very tired, almost delirious. He stopped at a closed gas station and used the washer fluid and squeegee near the pumps to wash the blood off the side of the car. It didn't look clean, but it didn't look like blood anymore either. There was nothing he could do about the broken windows. Around the back of the building he found a hose and rinsed himself off.

And then he climbed back in and drove some more. He wanted to get as far away from the temple, the half-bodies, the giant, the snap of Grida's neck as she died, as he possibly could.

He wondered about Artem. Once he had frozen and halved Grida, what would Artem do? Would he break down the door? Would he pound on it until one of the worshippers came to release him? Or would he simply lie down on the floor, his body arranged carefully, and wait to freeze to death?

Kline was so tired that after a while he could see not only his hand and arm gripping the steering wheel: he could also see, glowing, luminous, his missing arm gripping it as well. He watched, fascinated, trying not to become a believer, and nearly drove off the road. *I'm the devil*, he told himself, and drove, and drove.

EPILOGUE

1.

He awoke to the sunlight bright in his eyes, the air around him hot, his head feeling like it was splitting open. A police officer was standing beside his car, rapping on his windshield with one extended knuckle. Kline stirred, stared dumbly at him through the broken window.

"Mind telling me what you're doing here?" asked the officer.

"I," said Kline, "I was too sleepy to drive further. I thought it was safer to stop."

"That's commendable," said the officer. "Though it would have been even more commendable if you'd stopped at a hotel or in a rest area instead of on the side of the freeway."

"Yes, of course," said Kline. "Sorry."

"Where's your shirt?"

"I was hot with the windows on this side broken and the air rushing in," he lied. "It's in the back somewhere."

The officer glanced into the back. "It doesn't look like it's there," he said.

"It's probably on the floor," said Kline. "It's the same color as the floor mat."

Slowly the officer nodded. "Have you been drinking?"

"No, sir."

"Would you object to taking a Breathalyzer test?"

"Not at all."

The officer grunted, but made no move to get his Breathalyzer. "Mind showing me your driver's license?"

For a moment, Kline froze. What identity did he have that he could give to this man? But after the briefest hesitation, he smiled.

"Of course," he said. He worked the wallet he had taken from the half-body out of his pocket and began to thumb through it. There it was, a driver's license. The picture didn't look all that much like him, but wasn't out of the question. The height was right and hair color didn't matter much since most of his hair was gone. *Joseph Harkness*, the name was. He handed it over.

"Here you are, officer," he said.

The officer's gaze clung to his missing arm. The man had to make an effort to tear it away and look at the license. "Mr. Harkness," he said. "Wait right here, please. I'll be right back."

Kline watched the officer's back recede in the side mirror. Anything could happen, he told himself. Kline knew nothing about Joseph Harkness. Perhaps he was an upright citizen or perhaps he had a warrant out. It was a roll of the dice.

I'm done fighting, Kline thought. *If he wants to take me in, he can take me in.*

He sat in silence, waiting. Harkness was only the beginning, he realized. The officer would scan his plate too, or perhaps had already done so before waking Kline up. What would he find? Would he discover that this car was the last one an officer out near an old one-way bridge had called in before he had shown up dead? Had that officer actually bothered to call the plate in?

For a moment Kline found himself tempted to flee, but where would he go? *Maybe*, he thought, *I'm not done fighting after all.*

He leaned over and looked in the glove box, but the gun was no longer there. He had no knife, nothing he could use as a club. If worst came to worst, he'd have to kill the man with his bare hand.

He let out a deep sigh. Or maybe he would just let himself be taken.

For a long moment he waited, staring at the police car in the rearview mirror. And then the door opened and the officer stepped out and came back. His stride was slow, easy. Kline began to relax.

"Here you go, Mr. Kline," he said, and handed back the driver's license. This time Kline noticed that the man was missing half of his index finger. He stared at it, then looked up at the officer. *Kline*, he suddenly realized the officer, if he really was an officer, had called him.

He held very still.

The man stared hard at him, his eyes unreadable. "Have a nice day," he finally said, and walked back to his cruiser.

Probably the officer wasn't a full member of the Brotherhood. If he had been, he would have been missing the whole finger, not just the first two joints. No, he was not a member of the Brotherhood, but he was certainly a sympathizer. And he knew who Kline was, and would report back.

Indeed, the cruiser was following him, keeping its distance. He was being kept track of.

He ignored it, drove normally. If he tried to shake it, the officer could just turn on his flashers and pull him over. Even call for backup if he didn't stop.

There was no clear solution, and so the best thing to do, the only thing to do, was wait and see what would happen.

• • •

He couldn't drive forever. And yet, he didn't really have a place to go, either. He couldn't go back to his apartment, which must have been rented to someone else years ago. He had no friends alive he could turn to.

He went through the drive-thru of a burger joint, ordered, looked very carefully at the hands that passed him his bag through the window. All the digits were there.

In the parking lot, he disconnected the power wires and the car died. He ate a greasy burger topped with a slick layer of cheese. It tasted as good as anything he had ever eaten. He hadn't realized how hungry he was.

His fingers were still numb in places, as if they hadn't realized they were no longer in the cold, and as he lifted the burger to and from his mouth it felt like a small contingent of pins was traveling about beneath his flesh. The skin at the tips of his fingers looked waxen and had begun to flake away. A line of small blisters had begun to form, running from his wrist all the way up his forearm. He could tell from the throbbing in his feet and the soreness along the bow of his back that something was wrong there as well.

He finished the burger, crumpled the wrapper and dropped it into the bag. He could see, on the street, a half block down, the police cruiser waiting. *Where does someone go when there's nowhere to go?* he wondered. He couldn't stay in the car forever. He'd run out of gas soon, and the wallet he'd taken from what was left of Joseph Harkness had no credit card and very little money left with which to refill it. He couldn't stay on the streets or he'd be picked up. He couldn't go back to the shack he'd started out in, a few years back, the one where he'd been drinking himself to death. His friends and acquaintances were all dead. He had no one, nothing.

He reached down and touched the starter wire to the power wires. The engine turned over, caught. He put the car in gear, drove.

The booth looked just the same as it had before, the window casement repaired where the last guard had fallen through. There was nothing to suggest something bad had happened. Although Kline realized that, if you looked closely, you'd see the slight darkening on the concrete on the exit side of the driveway apron. They'd sprayed the blood away but hadn't scrubbed it out of the grain of the concrete.

He pulled up to the wrought-iron gate. When the car came near enough, it jerked once, then slid smoothly open.

Just beyond was the guard shack and barrier arm. He pulled up to it. The guard looked out the window. He appeared uncomfortable and strangely bulky. It took a moment for Kline to realize that this was probably because he was wearing a bulletproof vest.

"Can I help you?" asked the guard.

"I'm here to return a car," said Kline. "They're expecting me."

"Whose car?"

"P. Paul's."

The guard took a closer look at the car. He left the guard shack, came around to the front, wrote the license plate number down. Then he went back into the booth, picked up the phone. He stood there for a while, phone pressed to his face, and then leaned back out.

"Nobody's answering," he said.

"They've been having a problem with their phone," Kline lied. And then when the guard seemed skeptical, he added, "If they're not there, I can leave the car in the driveway and walk back out."

"I'm sorry," the guard said. "I can't let anyone I don't know through."

"Why not?"

"Policy," said the guard.

"It wasn't policy a few days ago," said Kline.

"Policies change," said the guard. He pointed to a sign that said *Property Under Surveillance*. "Also, we have cameras now."

Because of what happened to the other guard, he didn't say. "Can't you make an exception?" Kline asked. "I'm just returning a car."

"Where's your shirt?" asked the guard.

Fair enough, thought Kline. He looked like hell. Even if he recognized Frank's car, the guard would be a fool to admit him.

Kline threw the car into reverse. "Thank you for your time," he said. "Have a nice day."

He had only just backed up to the gate and was waiting for the guard to open it when the police cruiser appeared, blocking the drive behind. Kline considered ramming the barrier arm, but that would give both the security guard and the police officer reason to pursue him. He could reverse and ram the police car once the gate was open behind him, but he wasn't likely to get past, not before the officer drew his weapon.

The gate jerked, slowly began to slide open. Behind him the police officer got out of the car, came forward. He approached Kline's window, bent down.

"Having trouble, Mr. Kline?"

"He won't let me in."

"Do you want me to take care of it?"

Kline hesitated, nodded. As the policeman straightened, he added, "There are cameras now."

The policeman gave him a sharp look. "Why is that important?" he asked.

"I suppose," said Kline slowly, "it depends on how you intend to take care of it."

The man gave a smile. "Very good, Mr. Kline, very funny," he said, and then flicked the smile off.

He watched the officer and the guard conversing, the first standing on the drive, the second above him and leaning out the window. At one point the officer pointed back at Kline and the guard shaded his eyes to get a better look. The officer shrugged. He gestured with his hands a little and then both men laughed. A moment later they were shaking hands and the officer was heading back toward him.

"It's all settled," said the officer. "Have a nice day."

"Thank you," said Kline, by reflex.

"Just making sure you get to where you need to be, Mr. Kline. It's the least I can do."

In front of him the barrier arm lifted.

"Have a nice day," the officer repeated.

Kline drove through. He stopped a little way beyond the barrier arm, waited. In his rearview he saw the policeman get into his cruiser. He waited for the man to drive through as well, expecting him to come after him. Instead, he reversed out to the street, turned the wheel sharply and drove away. A moment later, the gate slid closed.

• • •

He drove slowly down the winding road, turned off onto the one-lane road, then counted out the three driveways on one side, the four on the other, before finally glimpsing the mailbox reading *P. Paul.* Kline turned into the driveway beside it, parked.

He went to the door, knocked. No answer. There was, he reminded himself, nobody left to answer. He checked it, found the door locked. There was a pebbled glass panel next to the door. Something was troubling him. He was unsure what. He kicked the panel in, kicked the shards of glass out of the frame, and then reached in deep enough to grab the doorknob and unlock it.

He was halfway down the hall before he realized what had been troubling him. He had been the last one to leave the house, and he had left the door unlocked. Which meant someone else had been here. And maybe still was.

He traced his way quietly back to the front door, closed it again. There was nothing to be done about the broken glass panel, and so he did nothing.

He went to the kitchen, plucked the butcher's knife out of the block. He stared at his elongated and warped reflection in it for a long moment, and then thought, *Enough.* He returned the knife to the block and climbed the stairs to Gous's makeshift office. The room was just as he had last seen it, except that the papers on the desktop were too neatly arranged, too orderly. In trying to give the impression of not having been there, whoever it was had overcorrected.

He walked down the hall to the nearest bedroom. He opened drawers until he found one full of T-shirts. He slipped a blue one on. It was too loose on him, but it would do.

He returned to Gous's office, closing the door behind him. He came around the desk and sat in Gous's chair. And then, facing the door, he waited.

The light slowly shifted its way across the room, then finally narrowed and faded, vanishing entirely. He didn't bother to turn on the light, just sat there in the dark.

It had been fully dark for a while, an hour perhaps, when he heard the front door open and close downstairs. They didn't seem concerned about staying quiet. Was that a good sign or a bad one? It could, after all, be the last remaining Pauls, coming home at last. But he doubted it.

He heard them moving about downstairs, talking to one another in voices that were low but far from whispers, and then he heard a voice say, louder this time, "He might have already left."

"Kline?" another voice shouted from below. "You here?"

Not the Pauls. Almost certainly the Brotherhood. He didn't say anything. They could come kill him if they wanted, but that didn't mean he had to make it easy for them.

There was more movement from downstairs, a cursory search of every room perhaps. And then he heard them come up the stairs, speculating aloud on where he might have gone. There were three voices, so at least three of them. A moment later, the door to the makeshift office opened and a hand reached in, flicked the light on.

"He's here," said someone standing in the doorway. He was a man with one eye, a beard, most of one arm covered by a machine gun prosthetic. A member of the sect of guards. Another guard appeared just behind the first, gun prosthetic pointed in the air. They filed in, eyes on him the whole time, one going left, the other right, each settling into a corner of the room. When they stopped moving, their gun prostheses had come to be aimed almost idly at Kline.

"Hand up," said the second guard.

"Do you have a weapon?" asked the first.

"No," said Kline. Slowly he lifted his hand.

"Why not?" asked the second guard. "Weren't expecting us?"

"Just the opposite," said Kline. "Because I expected you."

"Why should we believe you?" asked the first.

"You're welcome to search me if it'll make you feel any better."

They stared at him for a moment and then the one on the left's face slowly curled into a smile. "Clear!" he called.

There was a rustling in the hall. A moment later another man entered. He was tall, might have been handsome if it hadn't been for the fact that both ears and his nose had been cut away. One hand was missing entirely, the other had only a thumb and forefinger.

"Ah," the man said, his eyes bright. "Mr. Kline. We meet again at last."

"You must be DeNardo," said Kline.

The man smiled. All his teeth, Kline saw, had been removed. "How very perceptive of you, Mr. Kline," he said.

"You've come here to kill me," said Kline.

DeNardo shook his remaining finger at Kline. "Now, now, Mr. Kline, don't jump to conclusions. You don't know that for certain. If you begin with that assumption we won't be able to have a proper chat. Shall we say, instead, that I *might* kill you? That if I had my druthers I would prefer to let you live?"

"You're hoping to convert me. And if you fail in that, you'll kill me."

DeNardo gave a pained expression. "No need to state it so bluntly, Mr. Kline. You take all the delicacy out of what might best be described as a civilized chat between two intelligent and ruthless rivals who do not see eye to eye but who, if one of them is given proper persuasion, very well might."

The guards stayed motionless, guns always directed at Kline.

DeNardo cleared his throat. "Mr. Kline, I felt that the offer I extended to you by telephone was a little clumsily done. I wanted to extend it to you in person. And, in addition, if the information we have gathered has any validity—which it invariably does—circumstances have changed for you. Then, you had the Pauls to rely on. And yet no Pauls have returned to this house in the last few days. They seem to have simply vanished from the face of the earth! Perhaps they have been raptured up to heaven?" DeNardo leaned forward. "Of course, we both know that's very unlikely. And so, I wanted to ask you again, once more, for the final time, will you join us, Mr. Kline? Will you return to the fold?"

"I had an agreement with Ramse," said Kline.

"I'm sure you did," said DeNardo, his voice soothing. He looked around. "But I don't see Mr. Ramse here now, do you?"

"The agreement was made with the Brotherhood, through the person who was its leader. It would be wise for you as the head of the Brotherhood to acknowledge the agreement and honor it," said Kline, keeping his voice level.

For the first time, DeNardo seemed to lose his composure. "And why the hell would I want to do that?" he asked.

"So that the Brotherhood will survive."

DeNardo shook his head, gave a little laugh of frustration. "Do you think I'm a fool, Mr. Kline?"

"What was the deal?" demanded the first guard.

DeNardo spun and looked at him. The guard met his gaze calmly. "We should at least know," he said.

DeNardo sighed. "Oh, all right," he said, waving what was left of his hand. "Do tell us, Mr. Kline. Do inform us about the specifics of your so-called deal."

"It was simple. I agreed to leave him alone and he, in return, agreed to leave me alone."

"What you fail to understand here, Mr. Kline, is that I hold all the cards. I can make you do whatever I want."

"No," said Kline.

"No?"

"No," said Kline. "You can kill me, or can at least try to, but you can't make me do whatever you want."

DeNardo narrowed his eyes. "What do you mean, try to?" He turned to the guard on the right. "I thought you said he didn't have a weapon."

"He doesn't," said the guard.

"Why wouldn't we be able to kill you, Mr. Kline?"

Kline shrugged. "There's a number of people you could ask that question to, but they're all dead. And yet here I am, still alive."

"Yes," said DeNardo, "it's irritating, I admit, and somewhat confounding. But your luck has to run out sometime, Mr. Kline."

"What makes you certain that it will run out today?"

DeNardo guffawed. "You don't have a weapon, Mr. Kline. There are three of us. Two of us are members of the order of the guards and wear gun prostheses. What makes you think you can possibly survive?"

"I notice you're taking care not to come too close," said Kline.

"It's one thing to be confident, Mr. Kline, another thing to be foolhardy."

Kline said, "The right thing would be to honor the agreement that the Brotherhood made with me."

"The right thing! The honorable thing! These are mere words, Mr. Kline. Only power determines what is right and what is honorable and you have none of it. I ask you once again, one final time, to join us."

Kline pondered. His gaze flickered briefly from one to the other of the guards then came back to settle on DeNardo. "Is that why you felt you could kill the secret Paul that Gous sent to infiltrate you?"

"I can kill anyone I want," said DeNardo. "I'm in charge."

"Even though he was a guard? I thought I understood that the guards administer their own justice."

The guards' expressions didn't shift but they fell very still. DeNardo realized he had misstepped. "I didn't kill a guard," he said carefully. "I killed a Paul pretending to be a guard." But the guards remained still, attentive. *Good,* thought Kline.

"I feel that vows should be kept," said Kline. "Call me old fashioned that way. What can I sacrifice to prove to you that my vow to leave the Brotherhood in peace is serious?" asked Kline. "An eye perhaps?"

The two one-eyed guards behind DeNardo exchanged glances.

"I keep telling you, Mr. Kline, your agreement with Ramse means nothing at all. Ramse is no longer alive. Now, you must choose either to return to the fold, *my* fold, or die. To be honest, Mr. Kline, you're almost as much use to me dead as alive, and you're quite a bit less trouble. Now, your time is up. What do you choose?"

"I won't return to the fold," said Kline.

"No?" DeNardo looked incredulous. "Even though you know it will mean your death? What is wrong with you?" He waved his hand at the guards. "Well, there you have it," he said. "Some people you just can't talk sense into. Go ahead, kill him."

The guards aimed their gun prostheses at him. Kline closed his eyes, waited to die.

"An eye?" said the voice of the first guard.

Kline opened his eyes and stared steadily at him. "Yes," he said.

"What are you waiting for?" shouted DeNardo. "Kill him!"

For a moment the guard stayed staring at Kline, judging him, and Kline felt that things could go either way. Then he slowly swung his prosthetic gun to point at DeNardo.

"What are you doing?" said DeNardo, surprised.

"Some people still think promises are important," said Kline.

"But I didn't make the promise!" said DeNardo.

"Or maybe you shouldn't kill a guard without asking the other guards' permission first, whether he's a spy or not."

"Wait!" said DeNardo. "I can explain. I command—"

But the rest was cut off by the rattling of the guns. DeNardo's body shook, as if palsied, the bullets lodging inside it or thumping into the walls to either side of Kline. And then the rattling stopped and DeNardo's body slid to the floor.

Kline slowly stood and came around the desk. The guards' guns swiveled to follow him.

"Well?" the second guard said.

"Thank you," said Kline.

"A deal's a deal," said the first guard.

"Yes, of course," said Kline. "You and I both understand that. Let's go downstairs."

He walked toward the guards. They let him come without doing anything. He went past, his stride steady, slow, and out the door. He walked to the head of the stairs and went down them. The guards, he could hear, were following him.

In the kitchen he went to the knife block. He examined each knife in turn, wondering which would be the best. A steak knife would be okay, or a paring knife. An oyster knife would be ideal, probably, but there wasn't one in the block and if he started looking through the drawers they might think he was stalling. Who even knew if there was anything in the drawers? There was a peeling knife, though, with its beak-shaped blade. With that, he might be able to get it out in nearly one piece. He took the peeling knife out, held it loosely in one hand.

From the kitchen door, the two guards were watching him.

"Who will take over the Brotherhood?" Kline asked.

"What does it matter to you?" said the first guard. "You've vowed to leave us alone."

"The next leader will honor our agreement?"

"He will, if he wants to remain the leader," said the guard.

Kline nodded. He tested the blade of the knife with his thumb. It was sharp, cut smoothly, left a line that quickly filled with blood. But the tip of his thumb was dead from frostbite and he didn't feel it.

"How is this to be done?" asked Kline. "Any words that need to be spoken?"

"You made the promise," the first guard said. "You decide what needs to be said to seal it."

Kline nodded. He leaned against the counter. He took a deep breath. "I seal my vow to leave the Brotherhood be, and the Brotherhood seals its vow to leave me be. I do so here declare before these witnesses."

He started to lift the knife but then hesitated.

"I need someone to hold my eyelids open," he said.

The first guard gestured to the second, who moved forward and with the remaining fingers on his remaining hand spread Kline's eyelids. *If I wanted to kill him*, thought Kline, *this would be the moment*. He almost struck out. But that would be, he knew, a mistake, and almost certainly a fatal one.

He brought the knife up just to the rim of his eye. He breathed in deeply once, twice, a third time, and then worked the tip of the knife in between the orbit's rim and the eye, and then thrust and twisted hard.

The guard caught him as he fell, helped get him to a chair. For a moment his vision was maddened and he was able to see both forward and down at once, and then the knife found the nerve connections and cut them and he could only see with one eye and half of his head was seared through with pain.

Struggling not to faint, he dumbly watched the guards root around under the sink until they found a Ziploc bag. They scooped the eye into it, sealed it.

"The vow is sealed," said the first guard. "Though, if you decide to remove the other one, I'd recommend using a spoon."

"What are you going to do with my eye?" asked Kline.

"A reminder," said the guard. "For the guards only. Something for us to see. A protection for you in case another DeNardo ever comes along."

The second guard had gotten a washcloth and was pressing it to Kline's emptied eye socket. He pulled it away and Kline saw how it was soaked in blood and fluid. He put it in Kline's hand, folded his fingers around it, patted his shoulder, and then two guards went toward the kitchen door.

At the door proper, the first guard turned back. "We'll be waiting for you," he said. "Whenever you choose to fulfill your destiny."

"I never will," Kline managed. "And you promised to leave me alone."

"We will leave you alone. But we'll still be waiting," he said. And then they left.

He sat for a long moment, in pain, hours even. It was over then. It was finally over.

When the light began to change, when night began to end, he managed to get to his feet. He started toward the front door, but halfway there he stopped. After a few minutes, he turned around, went back. He made for the garage door instead.

He heard the humming of the freezer, felt its vibration through the garage door as soon as he touched the knob. He turned the knob. The steps down were remarkably hard to navigate without depth perception and while still in pain. He fell sprawling before he reached the bottom. He lay there for quite a while, wondering if the blood he was seeing on the floor beside him was from where he had gouged out his eye or from having struck his head. Probably both.

Eventually he made it to his feet. He stumbled to the freezer, pulled on the handle. There they were, the half-bodies. The freezer was nearly full, but if he pushed some bodies forward and others backward there was enough room for one more body.

He forced his way in and closed the door.

He stood there, the bodies on either side pressed against him, propping him up, and waited. He waited for the moment when he would begin to see their missing limbs and his own again, for the moment when, suddenly, he would be able to see again through the eye that was no longer there.

He settled into the cold, shivering.

It wouldn't be long now.

No hand bids me farewell. But at the corners and the very end of the street, in this purple dusk, a thousand severed hands float, fall, or withdraw with vegetal slowness.

—J. V. Foix, *Daybook 1918*
Lawrence Venuti, trans.

Coffee House Press began as a small letterpress operation in 1972 and has grown into an internationally renowned nonprofit publisher of literary fiction, essay, poetry, and other work that doesn't fit neatly into genre categories.

LITERATURE
is not the same thing as
PUBLISHING

Funder Acknowledgments

Coffee House Press is an internationally renowned independent book publisher and arts nonprofit based in Minneapolis, MN; through its literary publications, Coffee House acts as a catalyst and connector—between authors and readers, ideas and resources, creativity and community, inspiration and action.

Coffee House Press books are made possible through the generous support of grants and donations from corporations, state and federal grant programs, family foundations, and the many individuals who believe in the transformational power of literature. This activity is made possible by the voters of Minnesota through a Minnesota State Arts Board Operating Support grant, thanks to the legislative appropriation from the Arts and Cultural Heritage Fund. Coffee House also receives major operating support from the Amazon Literary Partnership, and the McKnight Foundation.

Coffee House Press receives additional support from Bookmobile; Dorsey & Whitney LLP; and the Schwab Charitable Fund.

MINNESOTA STATE ARTS BOARD
CLEAN WATER LAND & LEGACY AMENDMENT
amazon literary partnership
MCKNIGHT FOUNDATION

The Publisher's Circle of Coffee House Press

Publisher's Circle members make significant contributions to Coffee House Press's annual giving campaign. Understanding that a strong financial base is necessary for the press to meet the challenges and opportunities that arise each year, this group plays a crucial part in the success of Coffee House's mission.

Recent Publisher's Circle members include many anonymous donors, Patricia A. Beithon, Robin Chemers Neustein, Kelli Cloutier, Theodore Cornwell, Jane Dalrymple-Hollo, Jeremy M. Davies, Mary Ebert and Paul Stembler, Kamilah Foreman, Eva Galiber, Bryan Garrett, Roger Hale and Nor Hall, William Hardacker, Randy Hartten and Ron Lotz, Carl and Heidi Horsch, Amy L. Hubbard and Geoffrey J. Kehoe Fund of the St. Paul & Minnesota Foundation, Hyde Family Charitable Fund, Kenneth & Susan Kahn, the Kenneth Koch Literary Estate, Cinda Kornblum, the Lenfestey Family Foundation, Carol and Aaron Mack, Gillian McCain, Mary and Malcolm McDermid, Daniel N. Smith III and Maureen Millea Smith, Vance Opperman, Mr. Pancks' Fund in memory of Graham Kimpton, Alan Polsky, Robin Preble, Ronald Restrepo and Candace S. Baggett, Elizabeth Schnieders, Steve Smith, Jeffrey Sugerman and Sarah Schultz, Paul Thissen, Allyson Tucker, Grant Wood, Margaret Wurtele, Aptara Inc., The Buckley Charitable Fund, and Dorsey and Whitney Foundation.

For more information about the Publisher's Circle and other ways to support Coffee House Press books, authors, and activities, please visit www.coffeehousepress.org/pages/donate or contact us at info@coffeehousepress.org.

Praised by Peter Straub for going "furthest out on the sheerest, least sheltered narrative precipice," BRIAN EVENSON has won the World Fantasy Award, the International Horror Guild Award, and the Shirley Jackson Award. He is also the recipient of three O. Henry Awards, a Guggenheim Fellowship, and was a finalist for the Ray Bradbury Prize.

Phantom Limb was designed by Coffee House Press.
Text is set in Adobe Caslon Pro.